HOPE IN THE MOUNTAIN RIVER

CALL OF THE ROCKIES ~ BOOK 2

MISTY M. BELLER

Misty M. Beller

BOOKS

To Janet W. Ferguson,
So much more than a critique partner.

Your friendship, tough love, and never-ending support have been some
of the greatest blessings of my writing journey.
I'm so thankful God brought us together.

Therefore being justified by faith, we have peace with God through our Lord Jesus Christ:
*By whom also we have access by faith into this grace wherein we stand, and rejoice in **hope of the glory of God.***

Romans 5:1-2 (KJV)

CHAPTER 1

December, 1830
Bitterroot Mountains, Future Montana Territory

"*I*s he friend or enemy?" Elan's blood pounded through her veins as it did when the warriors from her tribe struck their targets with tomahawks—blow upon blow, louder and louder with each passing moment. She pulled her furs tighter around her shivering shoulders against the bitter wind whipping down the mountainside.

"I can't tell. They're..." Her faithful friend Meksem paused, then a tiny gasp slipped from her mouth in an icy cloud. "It's a *white* man." The shock in her voice thrust the words to a dangerously loud whisper.

"A French trapper?" Elan softened her own tone so she didn't alert the stranger of their presence. The trappers were the only *soyapo* who ever came to the Bitterroot Mountains. *White people*, they called themselves, from the northern country. She'd heard them speak of a place called Canada. Enough of these men had visited their camp that she'd become accustomed to their strange manners and learned some of their words.

"I don't know. There are two of them. No..." Another pause.

If only she had a clear view herself. Elan forced her legs to relax around her horse's sides. Everything in her wanted to ride the few steps forward beside her friend and peek through the trees to see the outsiders for herself.

But even that small movement could alert the strangers to their presence. Better to keep themselves hidden until they knew better what manner of persons they were up against.

With all her training among the braves, Meksem could likely protect the two of them from any harm these foreigners might plan. But sometimes stealth was a better feat than courage. Especially for two women alone in the mountains, facing white men who surely carried guns.

The emptiness in Elan's heart had stripped away any caution for herself, but for her friend, she had to be diligent. She couldn't lose Meksem—not to beast or man. Elan's eyes lifted to the angry gray sky. The coming weather couldn't be battled, though.

The clop of horses' hooves thumped loudly in the icy air as the strangers drew closer. There must be more than two traveling, as much noise as their animals created.

Finally, Meksem drew back from her perch among the cluster of trees and turned to face Elan. Instead of speaking aloud, she used the language of signs to share what she'd seen. *Four men and a woman.*

A woman? Elan's breath caught in her chest. These people must be friendly then. Unless the woman was a captive. She made the motions to ask, *All of them are white?*

Meksem shook her head, and her hands flew as she answered. *All but one man. He is not of The People. Not Shoshone either.*

Elan's heart stilled as fear clutched her throat.

Blackfoot?

Even as she signed the question, her mind revolted against

the answer. The Blackfoot were one of her people's most dangerous enemies. The stories of how they'd taken women and children captive and the awful way they'd treated them as slaves had been shared as warning in every lodge.

I don't know. Meksem's answer only stilled a small bit of the churning in Elan's middle. Maybe the man was Salish or from one of the other friendly tribes. After all, why would a Blackfoot brave be traveling so far south in the winter moons, especially traveling with a band of white people?

Her friend turned back to watch the strangers, and Elan braced herself for her first glimpse as the nose of a horse appeared between the trees. The moment Meksem had first caught the sound of riders approaching, Elan had spotted this perfect place to watch the strangers while keeping the two of them and their horses hidden.

The first sight she caught was of a horse with a long winter coat that had once been black, but long days in the sun had bleached the ends lighter brown. Its rider came into view, and something in Elan's middle tightened. He wore a fur coat and hat, much like the French trappers did, and she couldn't see much of his face except a glimpse of paler skin—the color of a white man's.

Yet something in his manner—maybe in his bearing, the way he sat atop his horse—struck a yearning inside her. He rode like a horseman, one capable of communing with his mount and moving as one. She'd seen this among some of the braves in their camp. After all, her people were known for their skill with horses and the unique spotted animals they raised. But she'd never seen a man who gripped her attention at first glance like this one.

When he'd nearly ridden past, she caught sight of the man riding behind him. This one truly did look like a Frenchman. Much like the trapper, Lebeau, who'd spent a winter in the lodge beside her own a few years back.

After the second man, a female passed by—a white squaw with light brown hair dressed in a beautiful set of buckskins and covered in a cape of fine wolf fur. She sat regally in the saddle—no mere serving girl, this one. Nor a captive.

Another horse climbed the trail close behind her, and the sight of raven hair poking out from under his fur cap made her chest tighten again. She couldn't see much of the man's face, only enough to agree that he was from one of the tribes. But which one?

The risk of showing themselves to find out wasn't worth any gain that might come from a meeting. Meksem knew the trail the two of them were following, as she'd passed through here several times on hunting trips, and they'd packed enough food to reach the great river. The only reason to reveal themselves would be curiosity to see what these people were about. Definitely not worth the risk.

After all, hadn't Elan chosen to take this journey to escape from people? Time alone was what she'd craved. Time to heal, if that were possible. Meksem knew how to keep silent and was an able guide and friend, so accepting her insistence on coming along hadn't been too hard.

Yet the long days of quiet hadn't eased the rending of Elan's body and heart yet. Nothing ever could. Not when her daughter's life had been crushed, ripped into bloody shreds by a single horrific act.

Chuslum had tried to save her. He'd done everything he could to rescue their only child. But his efforts hadn't been enough. No man could best a grizzly with only his hands, not even a brave as skilled as her husband had been.

Now, Elan was alone.

In one awful day, she'd been stripped of the two people who'd mattered most to her. How could she possibly go on? What was there without her child to give her life meaning?

Another man rode into view, bringing her focus back to the

present. This stranger sat taller than the others, almost bear-like wrapped in his furs. At least they'd all dressed suitably for travel through the deadly winter in these mountains. The snow only came above the horses' knees for now, but the low thick clouds meant more would be falling soon. This group must not have seen the cave they had to have passed early in the day, or they would have taken shelter. She and Meksem were riding hard to reach that cave before the worst of the snow came in a fury.

When the last pack horse marched past their hiding place, Elan forced her mind to focus on sounds around them. The horses' hooves crunching snow, the squeaking of saddles. One of the men murmured, but the group had moved far enough away that she couldn't make out the words. Not even what language it might be.

At last, silence descended over the land, settling on them like a heavy shroud. Pressing so hard she had to work to draw breath. Why did this quiet she'd craved now feel like the press of death?

Meksem turned, and her perceptive gaze roamed over Elan's face.

Elan turned away from her friend toward the eastern path they'd been riding. "Ready?"

Her friend nudged her mount forward. "If we ride hard, we'll reach the cave before the snow comes. This will be a deep one."

Meksem was right, no doubt. Yet the fury of the oncoming blizzard was nothing compared to the desolation left by the storm raging inside her.

~

*J*oel Vargas eyed the darkening sky overhead, then signaled for a halt as he reined his gelding in.

"That storm will strike any minute, no?" From

behind him, French peered up at the low clouds pressing down on them.

Joel scanned the rest of the group—Susanna, Beaver Tail, then Caleb in the rear. All these people he'd dragged into these treacherous Bitterroot Mountains. He'd expected the terrain to be rough—the cliffs steep and the footing dangerous. But he'd not expected the cold to be so fierce a man could freeze to death in an hour unless he bundled tight in furs.

And the snow already stood as high as the horses' knees. Now, they were about to get more? He'd never imagined such a place existed when he left Andalusia. The mountains in his Spanish homeland—at least where he and his brother had grown up—rose in majestic grandeur as these did, but the climate was so much more agreeable.

None of this frostbite and limbs so cold a man didn't dare make water until he first built a warming campfire.

"We passed a cave a few hours back. That would be a good place to wait out the storm." Beaver Tail spoke in his usual reserved manner.

Joel jerked his gaze to the man. "Why didn't you say something when you saw it?" And why hadn't Joel seen it himself? How did Beaver always manage to be one step ahead, even when Joel did his best to keep every one of his senses alert?

Beaver sent a glance around them, ever watchful. "I didn't think you'd want to wait half a day just to keep from riding in snowflakes."

The pressure in his chest pinched harder. Did his friends think him such a dictator he would risk their lives just to make a half-day's progress in their trek?

Yes, this journey was important. Every half day could mean life or death for his brother—the brother he hadn't seen in over a year now. He didn't actually *know* if Adam was in danger. He only suspected so because Adam's note had said he'd find Joel in the summer. About five months ago.

While Joel had no certain knowledge of Adam's peril, he *did* know this snowstorm could be the death of them all if they didn't find proper shelter and a dry place for a fire.

Reining his horse around, he nodded toward Caleb. "Let's retrace our steps. We won't find Adam if we all turn to icicles."

The next hours dragged on as the temperature dropped. Not even the majestic views surrounding them—peaks rising up like cathedrals into the clouds—could overcome the miserable cold.

"Behind those two boulders just ahead of you." Beaver Tail's voice broke the interminable silence.

Joel craned his neck to see the cave his friend had spotted. He rode in the back of the line now, so he didn't get a glimpse of the opening until the others had reined their horses in a semi-circle around the spot.

Two stones stood as tall as men, palace guards in front of the cave's entrance, permitting access only through the narrow space between them. He could see why most people wouldn't notice the dark hole hiding behind the rocks.

But *he* should have seen it. He'd spent his life watching for danger, trying to spot potential hazards and possible protection. How had he missed this?

Beaver Tail had already dropped to the ground and padded forward to slip between the stone barriers. Ever the scout and protector.

Joel gripped his rifle as he slid from his own mount and stepped forward to follow his friend. Surely Beaver knew the chance that a bear or other animal had taken refuge inside, but just in case, Joel asked the question. "Think anything is in there?"

Beaver didn't even slow, just tipped his chin to throw his voice back to Joel. "Mayhap."

He was prepared then.

With the gun in Joel's left hand, he gripped the hilt of his knife with his right and followed his half-Blackfoot friend through the boulders. Joel could shoot a gun with decent aim, but he'd spent so many long hours on the ship from Andalusia perfecting his skills with a blade, he'd be quicker with that weapon in an attack.

Beaver Tail slipped into the darkness of the cave without a pause, even though the interior yawned black. Joel pulled out his knife, but kept the blade pointed downward as he used the fist of that hand to feel the air in front of him. Better not to run into anything.

Every one of his senses strained to hear a sound or catch a whiff of odor, something other than the dank scent of damp stone and decaying leaves. Even a shifting of shadows.

The low growl of Beaver Tail's voice was his first alert. "Show yourself."

Joel's chest tightened as he strained to hear or see the threat Beaver had sensed. He could make out Beaver's form now that his eyes were adjusting to the dim interior. But only darkness lay beyond.

Beaver's voice hadn't echoed through the space, so this cave must not be large. Joel stretched his right hand—the one gripping the knife—sideways as far as he could reach to see if his knuckles brushed the rock wall.

His hand touched fur, and he nearly jumped even as he jerked his hand back.

At the same moment, a tiny squeal—a gasp, really—filled the air.

A shuffle sounded in front, just as a hard body slammed into him.

CHAPTER 2

*J*oel stumbled backward, trying to keep his feet underneath him, jerking his arms to pull free of the attacker pressing them to his side.

Another blow struck, as if something had hit the creature on top of him. The harder push knocked aside what little balance he'd regained, and he landed hard on his rear.

Then the body on him peeled away. A hiss filled the air, then an almost cat-like yelp. But not a cat.

Human.

The sounds of deep grunts and higher squeaks tumbled among heavy breaths. Beaver must be struggling to overpower whoever or whatever had attacked them. Joel scrambled to his feet and adjusted his grip on his knife. But in the darkness, all he could see were tangling shadows.

A voice rose above the din, shrieking a string of sounds he couldn't understand, but their forcefulness filled the air. The higher strains of a woman's voice couldn't be denied.

The scuffling sounds quieted. In fact, the cave grew so quiet, Joel's breathing seemed the only noise to be heard. That and the pounding of his pulse.

Then Beaver Tail's voice emerged, low and guttural. The sounds he made didn't combine into any of the Blackfoot words Joel had learned the last winter they'd spent among Beaver's people. Did he know the language the woman had spoken?

Quiet again settled over them. Then a responding voice. A woman, as he'd thought, and she spoke only a few words that Joel couldn't understand.

Then another voice spoke up—also a woman—and it sounded as though she stood within arm's reach on his right. She must be one he'd touched. But not the one who'd attacked him?

Beaver responded in the same language, although his words seemed slower and halting. Maybe he didn't know that tongue as well as the women.

For once, something the man didn't excel at. No matter that Beaver spoke fluent Blackfoot, French, English, and the sign language all the mountain tribes used. For Joel's part, he could only claim a few Spanish dialects, English, and a spattering of French, along with the signs and Blackfoot words Beaver had taught them. Not shabby, but not good enough to understand what was being said now.

The volley of conversation paused, and Beaver switched to English. "We will all go outside to speak more easily." A hint for Joel to lead the way, no doubt. He stood closest to the opening, after all.

Joel stepped backward, turning a little so he could walk without running into anything but also keep an eye on the shadowy figures coming behind him. He wanted a look at these two women the moment they reached daylight.

As he stepped out of the cave, he didn't glance at his friends, who'd surely heard the scuffle. If he had to guess, he'd bet three rifles were trained on them now—French's, Caleb's, and Susanna's. Beaver Tail's new wife wasn't one to back down when any of them needed defending. Especially if that person was her new husband.

Which made him wonder. Did anyone else hide inside the cave? Maybe an injured brave belonging to one of these women? He'd need to be on the alert.

As he eased backward between the stones, the first stranger stepped into the light. He wasn't sure what he'd been expecting, but the Indian woman who appeared stole his breath. Maybe the white-gray fur draping her shoulders gave her a regal look, or maybe the bold lift of her chin bespoke an Indian princess. But those eyes were what really drew him. Dark and expressive. Soft, yet impossible to read.

She met his gaze, and something there drew him. A longing. A sadness. An utter lack of fear, despite the fact that she was very much at the mercy of strangers. An invisible hand gripped his chest and twisted, stealing his breath.

Another figure stepped from the cave behind her, and Joel shifted his gaze just enough to see that this second woman looked about the same age as the first, maybe early in her twenties. Not far from his own three and twenty years.

The second female wore a red mark on her forehead, which might be blood, and anger on her face severe enough to shoot arrows in them all.

Joel edged out of the narrow place between the boulders, as much to slide away from that glare as to allow the women to come out of the cramped space.

Beaver Tail emerged from the cave and motioned the women forward. As Joel had suspected, the others stood with their horses in a semicircle, long barrels aimed at the women.

Susanna's gun lowered a little, and a frown settled on her face as she studied the women, then raised her focus to her husband.

Beaver looked perfectly composed and uninjured, as if he'd

not just scuffled with two Indians in the darkness. Probably not even breathing hard.

Beaver Tail addressed the women using signs, and Joel narrowed his focus to the sweep of the man's hands. He could pick out a few motions, enough to piece together some of the questions. But Beaver was also kind enough to speak the English translation as he made each motion.

"Question, you travel with?" He dropped the small words and arranged his spoken words in the same order as each sign, just the way he'd done when teaching them the language.

The second woman, the one who emanated fierceness, responded with her own gestures. *We travel to great river.* She pointed east as she spoke, maybe toward the Missouri?

Beaver's gaze flicked to French. "Light some tender and see if anyone else is in the cave."

"None." The first woman spoke, the one with the intriguing eyes. The single English word carried a heavy accent, but she must have understood what Beaver Tail said.

Beaver didn't look surprised, just nodded and glanced at French again. "Get a campfire started."

Good thing Beaver hadn't asked Joel to do it. He would have hated to miss whatever would be spoken here. His friend probably knew that.

"Question, your names?" Beaver directed his signs to both women, still accompanying them with spoken English. Maybe that was for his wife's benefit, although he'd probably been teaching Susanna both his native Blackfoot tongue and the language of signs.

Pretty Eyes pointed to herself. "Elan." Then at her friend. "Meksem." Both words rolled off her tongue in a musical cadence, making him want to ask another question, just to keep her talking.

Beaver Tail did the job for him. "You are Nez Perce?"

Joel's pulse leapt at the name. Maybe they knew Adam. With

all the chaos of their meeting, he'd not thought about a possible connection to his brother.

Elan nodded. "Ni-mee-poo."

Something flicked across Beaver's face—an expression like annoyance. Only a flash, but it snagged Joel's curiosity. "What did she say?"

Elan turned to him, her expressive eyes holding a hint of pride. "The People."

"Nez Perce is a name given them by French trappers." Beaver spoke almost underneath his breath. "They call themselves The People."

"You are Blackfoot?" The other woman spoke this time, her eyes flashing with something stronger than dislike.

Beaver Tail gave a single nod. "I mean you no harm."

Joel glanced among the three of them. If he was reading this right, there must be some kind of bad blood or mistrust between the two tribes. Beaver had never hinted at such, but Joel would have to ask about it later.

For now, large snowflakes had begun to fall, and Caleb had started to unload their animals and carry supplies into the cave. They all needed to make camp. As much as he wanted to question these women about his brother, that would have to wait until they and the animals were settled.

"Do you have horses?" Joel directed his question to both women, but his gaze honed in on Elan. He couldn't seem to stop himself.

The other woman—her name had been so unusual, he hadn't quite caught the sounds—grunted, and a look passed between the two.

"We won't hurt you or take your animals." Joel did his best to make his tone sound friendly, not intimidating in the least. "A storm is coming. We need to make sure all the horses are safe."

Elan pointed around the curve of the mountain and made the sign for *trees*. They must have found shelter for them.

Beaver shot him a glance. "Susanna and I will settle our horses with theirs. None of the animals will fit through those boulders to get in the cave, so we'll have to drape them with furs." His expression clearly added, *Can you and French and Caleb make sure these two don't run off?* Beaver surely didn't plan to keep these women hostage, but with the storm coming on, the cave would be the safest place for them all.

Joel nodded and motioned the women toward the entrance where a faint glow showed French had made progress with a fire. "Let's go in."

~

*E*very one of Elan's senses stood on alert as she followed Meksem back into the cave. The white man with the dark eyes followed behind her. Being surrounded by so many strangers should course fear through her, but this wasn't terror thrumming through her veins.

Apprehension, yes. And maybe a bit of worry. But, in truth, she hadn't felt this alive in months. Not since her world shattered.

Perhaps excitement was what she'd needed.

Since a woman traveled with these four men, they probably weren't a war party. Of course, sometimes a woman played the part of a warrior—Meksem was an example of such. But the woman who'd exchanged a long look with the Blackfoot brave wasn't dressed as a warrior.

The man behind Elan motioned to the ground beside the fire another man was nurturing. "Sit."

She'd picked up a few of the white men's words from the trappers who came through their village, which meant she could understand their language better than she could find the words to respond.

She and Meksem obeyed, dropping to sit on their heels, a

position they could both rise from quickly if needed. Beside her, Meksem looked to be coiled tighter than a wildcat preparing to spring. In fact, she almost lunged when the man building the fire stood unexpectedly.

Elan didn't catch all his quick-spoken words but did understand *wood*. Another man entered after that one left, and the newcomer loomed massive in the dim space. Maybe the two saddles and many packs loading his shoulders made him look larger than he really was. But when he dropped his burdens beside the cave wall and turned to go back out, his broad frame hadn't lessened in stature. His face tipped in a friendly nod as he stepped past them.

The other man—the one with the dark eyes who'd followed them in—moved to the load that had just been deposited and began pulling out bundles. Finally, she had a moment to watch him unhindered.

His movements were all quick, yet smooth. As though he knew exactly what he meant to do and wasted no action. Did she dare ask his name?

Maybe if he came closer to them again.

The Frenchman building the fire returned with an armload of sticks and dropped them in a noisy clatter on the floor. This was something she could do if they'd allow her.

She rose on her knees and reached for one of the driest logs, keeping her movements slow and without any sign of threat. He stepped back and watched her as she positioned the wood on the small fire to feed the tiny flame.

After a long moment, he spoke again, then turned and walked out of the cave. The man working with the supplies sent her a glance at the same time she'd looked his way. Their eyes snagged. Not what she'd intended at all, but it gave her a chance to read whether these men meant them harm.

His dark gaze shimmered in the low flicker of firelight, making his thoughts hard to determine. Curiosity maybe?

Interest for certain. No malice shone in his eyes. In fact, despite the intensity in his every motion, something about him soothed her.

The sensation drew a yearning inside her she hadn't felt in many moons. And she knew better than to allow the feeling now.

Elan dropped her gaze as she reached for another piece of wood. Better not to draw attention to herself. She'd really like to know this dark-eyed man's name, though.

The big fellow entered with another load, and she was careful to only watch from the edge of her vision as he dropped the pile of bundles and went back outside. When quiet again settled over the place, the dark-eyed stranger rose to his feet and moved toward them.

He crouched beside the fire and held out a strip of buckskin holding what looked like roasted meat. Her belly tightened at the savory scent rising to her nose. They'd not eaten since the camas bread at sunrise.

"Eat." He laid the bundle on the stone floor, then eased back, staying crouched as he watched them. "I am Joel." He pointed to his chest, and thankfully, he spoke the words slowly enough she could make them out.

A thrill slipped through her as her mind replayed the name. *Joel.* Strong and rhythmic. Intense, just like him.

The fire-builder stepped back into the cave, and Joel pointed up at him. "He is called French."

Over a load of wood, the man tipped his lips in a grin. She couldn't make out what he said, but his expression stayed friendly.

Joel motioned to the meat again. "Eat." Then he rose and stepped back, taking the unnerving weight of his presence with him.

CHAPTER 3

*A*s the three men worked around them, Elan nurtured the fire and eyed the food, but she didn't touch it, no matter how the meat's savory scent beckoned her. Finally, she glanced at Meksem and gave her a look that asked what she thought of the food. Her friend's glare almost pulled a smile from Elan. Of course Meksem would expect the worst. Always the protector.

Just to tease her friend, she reached for a small piece and raised it to her mouth. The scent grew so strong, she wouldn't have been able to make herself drop the meat if she'd wanted to. Her stomach ached with hunger. Her teeth sank into the fare, savoring the strong flavor of buffalo. She'd not had anything other than camas root and salmon since before she and Meksem had left on this journey, almost two moons before. Back when the first winter snow had barely covered the well-trod ground in their village.

As she took her second bite, she reached for another chunk of meat and handed it to Meksem. Her friend's glare took on the look of a grumpy child, but she accepted the food. Meksem knew better than to pass up sustenance, especially fare as flavorful as this.

When the Blackfoot man and his woman stepped into the cave, the space seemed to shrink. With all of them in this tiny cavern, so many figures moving around, casting shadows on the wall, part of her wanted to jump up and run for fresh air. No matter that snow fell heavily outside and the icy shriek of wind howled through the mountain pass.

After dropping her load against the wall with the other things, the woman turned and lowered herself to her knees in front of the fire. She smiled at them as she pulled off her gloves and extended her hands to the flame. "*Hóó.*"

Elan couldn't keep the surprise from her face at the greeting in their own language. "Hello."

The woman's cheeks and nose were bright red from cold. "I'm Susanna." She'd changed back to her own language and now spoke another string of words, but Elan could only pick out *meet.* But the friendliness in her tone—even pleasure—couldn't be misunderstood.

The kindness tugged at something in Elan that had lain dormant for so long, the sensation felt foreign.

Susanna paused and looked to be waiting for them to answer. Elan replayed the last few sounds the woman had spoken but couldn't decipher their meaning. If only she'd tried harder to learn the language.

Disappointment shadowed Susanna's face as she realized neither of them understood her. She looked over at her husband and said something. Elan caught the word *speak.* Maybe she was asking for help?

The brave looked at her, not sparing a glance for Elan or Meksem. His eyes softened in a way she wouldn't have expected, making him look less the fierce enemy warrior. That look bespoke a love like Elan had always craved, and the burn that surged up her throat and nipped at her eyes forced her to look away.

There were times she thought she'd seen that look in Chuslum's eyes. A few times...especially in their early days together. But now she'd never know for sure.

The Blackfoot man came to kneel beside his wife, facing Elan and Meksem. Susanna spoke to him, then he addressed them in sign language, speaking in the white man's tongue with each motion. "My squaw is happy to see you." He pointed to them. "Friends."

Susanna's smile flashed bright teeth, making her beauty even more striking. "Yes. Friend." She made the same sign, then grinned at them. This woman was impossible not to like.

Joel came to kneel beside the Blackfoot man, nearer Elan than he'd been before. He carried a sweet, musky scent that made her want to lean in. He looked from her to Meksem, then back to her. "We're looking for my brother." He spoke in the white tongue, but slowly enough that she captured almost every word—at least enough to fill in the gaps. For some reason his cadence was easier to understand than the others.

He pointed to his face. "He is like me. Dark hair. His eyes..." He spoke a word she didn't understand, but she'd caught enough of the rest to know she wouldn't be able to help him.

She shook her head. "See no white man." Just in case she had the words wrong, she used signs, as well.

The light in his eyes dimmed, and even though he'd not been exactly smiling before, the pleasure slipped from his face. "You're certain?"

She heard his words, but wasn't familiar with the second one. But the lingering threads of hope in his eyes made his meaning clear. She shook her head again. "No white man." For his sake, she wished they had.

Joel nodded, resignation cloaking his face.

The Blackfoot man began signing again, and she pulled her focus from Joel to catch everything he said.

We seek his brother who travels with Shoshone. They look for the spotted horses. Spotted horses Elan's tribe had aplenty. In fact, the mounts she and Meksem rode possessed the special blend of white spots on dark base coat that her people raised.

Her friend didn't look like she planned to answer, so Elan responded. *You are traveling the Lolo trail?* Meksem knew most of the paths that made up that trace, probably better than any Shoshone would. But the two of them were traveling the opposite direction, toward the great river where the buffalo roamed.

Still, maybe Meksem would be able to give them direction if they needed help.

The Blackfoot nodded. Perhaps she should ask his name, but she was still struggling to see him as anything other than an enemy to fear.

So many times, Blackfoot raiding parties had attacked her people, stealing possessions and taking captives. She could still remember the keening of her mother's friend when her almost-grown daughter had been stolen in a bloody attack. The girl had been so innocent, the thought of what she suffered at the hands of her captors roiled in Elan's middle, churning up anger toward all of those people.

Was this man any different? He'd not been brutal in his handling of them, and he seemed kind to his squaw. Real affection seemed to exist between them.

She'd have to do her best to keep from judging him until she saw more.

As his hands moved again, she focused on the gestures. *Do you know which way they would have gone? Is there a place where most of the spotted horses are kept?*

She glanced at Meksem. Maybe she shouldn't speak freely to these strangers, but their intentions seemed innocent. "Our village has many. And I can think of two or three more. All are across the mountains." She pointed west, back the way they'd come.

Meksem only nodded, clearly not intending to add anything more. She must still be angry that this man had bested her in the dark. In another place and time, Elan might have smiled at her sullenness. Maybe even goaded her into laughing at her own childishness.

But Elan hadn't been able to laugh for so long now. How could she manage to pull that reaction from anyone else?

She turned to the brave to see if he'd understood her words. He was looking at Joel, and she caught a long glance between them. A conversation without words, and she could easily read Joel's part.

He wanted the Blackfoot man to ask her and Meksem to lead them to her people. To the places where his brother might have gone seeking the Palouse horses.

The churning in her middle pulled into a tight knot. Could she turn back so soon? The great river likely lay only ten or twelve sleeps ahead. She'd almost reached her goal. At least, her spoken goal.

But in truth, the river had only been an excuse. She'd had to get away from the place where everything reminded her of Alikkees. Away from the lodge where she'd nursed her sweet baby and taught her to walk and talk. Away from the dreams she'd had for her daughter and all the things she would teach her. All the stories she and Alikkees made up, taking turns imagining what life would be like as one of the elk or birds or fish swimming in the rivers.

She wasn't ready to go back. She couldn't face that place again, not yet.

But a glance at Joel and the yearning in his eyes loosened the knot in her belly. Could she do it for him? Why was it so urgent he find his brother?

She spoke in sign so they would have a better chance of

understanding her. *The mountains are not good to travel in the snow. Many do not keep the trail. Many die. You should wait until the snow melts and The People ride the spotted horses across the mountain to hunt buffalo.*

Joel studied her motions with even more intensity than his usual manner, and even when she finished, he remained motionless, his brow furrowed in concentration, as though he was still deciphering her gestures.

At last, his expression eased, and his gaze flicked up to hers. "You said you think we should wait until spring when the snow melts?" He spoke his own language, and she had to strain to understand, the same way he had with the signs. From what she could gather, he'd comprehended her comments well.

She couldn't help a little smile for him as she nodded.

But his frown returned. "My brother has been missing. I need to find him. He needs help. Can you take us to your people so I can find him?"

Maybe she didn't understand exactly what he was saying, for his words left her with many questions, but the worry in his gaze couldn't be denied. An urgency hung around him that could only come from fear.

She knew that fear. She'd felt it the day Chuslum didn't return with their daughter when he'd said he would. As the sun had passed through the sky, fear had clutched her by the throat, tainting the air she breathed just as it did now with Joel. She'd known something was wrong with her dearest ones, but she'd not been able to reach them until too late.

From the desperation in his eyes, Joel fought that same fear. Could she let herself be the one to keep him from his brother until it was too late?

She looked to Meksem. Her perceptive friend was watching her, an understanding in her eyes. This was why she loved her. This was why she'd allowed her to come on this journey. "We must." She spoke the words quietly, not much more than a whisper.

The Blackfoot might understand her, and maybe he planned to force them to be guides anyway, but this was the moment for them to choose which route they would willingly follow.

Something within her said taking Joel to his brother would be more important than the journey to the river could ever be.

~

*J*oel's gut twisted in ten different knots as he watched the interchange between the women. Something told him they were the key to finding Adam. Maybe the thought was only him grasping for hope, but it felt more like instinct.

Just like the instinct that told him Adam was in trouble.

Elan and her friend *had* to agree to guide them through these treacherous mountains and to Nez Perce camps where the Palouse horses were. Places Adam might have gone. Joel didn't have time for any delays.

At last, Elan turned to him, the expression on her face impossible to read. Even her eyes, which had been so expressive before, now shifted to a look he couldn't decipher.

Then she locked her gaze on his, and for a long second he couldn't breathe. She nodded, and the coil in his chest eased as if the boulder settled there had finally been pushed away.

She spoke words he couldn't understand, but that nod had been the language of his heart.

Beaver Tail was gesturing in signs to them, and Joel had to force himself to focus. His mind wouldn't listen, though, spinning with its own questions. How long would it take to cross the mountains?

And the more immediate question…how long before this snow stopped so they could set out?

CHAPTER 4

"*I* don't like it."

Elan cut her eyes to Meksem before mounting her horse the next morning. "Lower your voice." They'd not had much chance to speak alone through the night, as small as the cave had been and as many people had been packed inside.

"We should go to the river like we planned. Like you wanted to." Meksem settled on her own spotted mare. "Can you explain to me why we should help these men?"

"There's a woman with them too." She couldn't help a sly grin.

Meksem rolled her eyes. "I suppose that's a good reason."

Elan shrugged. "I wouldn't want her life on my hands."

"Her thieving husband will look after her."

"Meksem." Elan infused a warning in her tone. "He seems like a decent sort. You can't judge him based on the tribe he's from."

"We'll see." She nudged her mare forward to ride alongside Elan as they made their way around the cluster of rock to where the rest of the group waited. "That other one, the black hair, looks like a better sort. Don't you think?"

Her voice held an undertone that prickled Elan's guard. "A better sort for what?"

Meksem hummed a sound that raised Elan's ire even more. She turned a glare on her friend. "Leave it be. He seems like a good man but nothing more than that."

Meksem dipped her head, and her expression turned so apologetic, regret wove through Elan's belly. Maybe she shouldn't have been so harsh, but what Meksem hinted at—if what Elan was feeling were real, if she gave in to those feelings, then it would be like turning her back on the family that had been everything to her.

Even the thought made her want to retch. She'd had a daughter she loved and a husband happy for her to make his home, but they'd both been stripped away. Her entire life shattered in a single day. She would never, *ever* let herself be so vulnerable again.

They rounded the stone and halted when they reached the others. The Blackfoot—Beaver Tail, he was called—was holding Susanna's horse as she mounted. The other men already sat atop their horses. Joel was speaking with French but glanced her way with his dark eyes, which seemed to see everything.

The happy leap of her heart when she saw him was a sensation she'd not felt in so long. One she shouldn't feel. She pressed the sensation down and shifted her focus to the landscape around them. Snow had coated the branches with a fresh layer, deepening the path so the horses had to lift high hooves to trudge through.

Soon enough, they all set off with Meksem in the lead, following the trace the two of them had traveled the day before. A knot twisted in her chest at the thought of returning home.

But just because she was returning to the village didn't mean she had to stay there.

After Joel was reunited with his brother, she'd be free to leave. Did she dare risk the mountains again during the hardest winter months? Meksem would probably insist on coming too, and she couldn't put her friend in such danger. Not with snow and ice built up as high as the horses' bellies over the steep peaks they'd have to maneuver.

She'd gladly risk her own life—there was no one left to mourn her. But she couldn't jeopardize Meksem or the horses. So maybe she'd go south. Or west down the river, toward the great water she'd heard of.

Or better yet, maybe they'd find Joel's brother before reaching her village and she wouldn't have to face the memories after all. She could ride a wide circle around the land of her people and follow the rivers to the great water.

A thought slipped in, and she nudged her mare up beside Meksem. "We didn't meet Shoshone braves on our way. Should we take a different path back in case we can catch up to them?"

Meksem didn't answer at first, but her brows dipped in the middle in the way only her friend could manage, a sign she was pondering the question. "We can."

Elan nodded. A gust of wind swept through the trees and worked icy fingers under her fur hood. She ducked deeper into her wrap and let her horse fall back into line.

As they wound down the hillside, the next cliff rose ahead of them, steep and majestic with its sheer stone faces peeking out through white-covered crags. They would need to wind around the side of that mountain, scaling almost to the top because of the peaks so close on either side.

Her belly knotted as she remembered the sensation of standing at the very top of the world, feeling as though a single step forward would topple her over the edge. Even now she could imagine the empty air beneath her. Falling, falling. Sharp rocks jutting out to slow her tumble. The slam of solid stone and the awful crack of bone as her life faded into nothingness.

She closed her eyes and clutched her horse's mane as she fought to push the images aside. She didn't want that. Death was not better. She had to find a new way to live. Something more to live for.

Inhaling a long, deep breath, she imagined the icy air soaking through her body, filling her with strength. With determination.

At last, she opened her eyes. She did have a purpose—to help Joel find his brother. She would seek the man out to the four corners of the earth if she had to. No matter what the search required of her, she would fulfill this mission. After that, she didn't know what she'd do with herself.

But at least for now, she had something to live for.

~

*J*oel was surprised at how hard Meksem drove them. No matter how much the wind whipped up icy crystals and the exhausted horses floundered through the deep snow, she never slowed.

They'd eaten in the saddle, only stopping three times for the horses to catch their breath. Twice, they'd dismounted to walk a while so the animals could rest and the people regain circulation in their benumbed feet.

Even now as dark came on, the woman didn't show any sign of stopping to set up camp.

He was more desperate than any of them to keep moving and find his brother, but even *he* knew riding these steep trails after dark would be dangerous.

"Meksem." He raised his voice so she could hear him over the howl of the wind.

She glanced back, her face a tawny oval outlined by her fur hood.

He gave the sign for a halt, and she finally pulled her horse to a stop. He nudged his gelding out of line to ride up to her. With stiff, glove-covered fingers, he tried to make the sign for camp.

The woman didn't answer, just stared at him. Maybe trying to decipher what he meant.

"You want camp?" Elan spoke softly from beside her friend.

He nodded. She seemed much better at English, and, apparently, she could read clumsy signs too. "We need to stop." He pointed to the dusky sky. "Dark."

Their female slave-driver spoke a string of words to her friend in their own tongue. Elan turned to him again. "No food for horses. Ride long now while have strength."

His mind spun as he processed her meaning. True, there hadn't been a blade of grass for the horses to eat since early the day before. They'd fed the animals a little cornmeal the night before. But none of them had expected there to be no fodder at all for their mounts. "How long until we find food for the animals?"

"Four sleeps. Five sleeps."

Four or five days? The animals would be weak and exhausted by then, not able to carry their riders over this steep terrain.

"Ride long now." Elan spoke again.

He nodded. What they said made sense. They should cover as much ground as they could while the animals had energy. But wouldn't it be dangerous to travel the treacherous mountains in the dark?

"Will it be too dark to see?" He made the signs for *night* and *see*.

Elan shot a glance at her friend, then back at him. He might be mistaken in the dim light, but her eyes seemed to hold a twinkle. "Meksem sees like cat. Show us good way."

Meksem must be some kind of lady warrior, as well-versed in the ways of the woods as any brave. She reminded him a little of Beaver Tail.

He had to bite back a grin at that thought. His friend

wouldn't much like being compared to this woman, whose look said she didn't trust or much like the Blackfoot brave.

"All right." He nodded to Elan. "Ride on." They'd chosen to put faith in these women, and their wisdom seemed sound.

He could only hope he didn't regret the decision.

Night had come on in full for at least an hour before they finally stopped to make camp. He hadn't thought the temperature could plunge any colder, but the wind rushing around the mountain had frozen him to his very core.

Thankfully, Meksem halted them in a dip between mountains, where a massive boulder blocked the wind and offered an edge of ground protected from snow. One of the packhorses carried dry wood, but he'd not thought it possible to get a fire going with the wind whipping so hard. In this sheltered area, maybe—just maybe—they could thaw frozen limbs.

He and the other men had developed a routine to set up camp, and Susanna had found her own place in the procedures, usually unstrapping the main food pack and starting meal preparations while Caleb built a fire. French would unload the rest of the supplies while Joel and Beaver Tail settled the horses for the night.

Since there wasn't any grass for the animals, they set up a tie line near the boulder, then covered the horses with furs and fed them a small amount of cornmeal. The tiny bit they had to offer seemed cruel when the mounts had worked so hard all day, but there was so little to go around. They had to save enough for a handful each evening. If only they'd known the going would be so hard for the animals on this trail through the mountains, maybe they could have gathered grass to bring along.

He wasn't surprised when Elan worked with Susanna over the food and Meksem saw to their two horses. Something in Elan's expression made him think she was the nurturing type. Her face held a sweetness, despite the sadness that shadowed her beautiful eyes. If she ever truly smiled, he had a feeling her features would glow with a beauty that exceeded most women's. Even imagining the sight made his stomach flip.

But that line of thought would only get him in trouble. He had a brother to find, and getting himself tangled with a woman was the last thing he needed.

As he unstrapped the packsaddle from the last of their horses, he couldn't help but slide his gaze over to the two spotted mares the women rode. With their striking patches of color, no wonder their fame had spread all the way down the Missouri River.

Had Adam found any Palouse horses like these yet? Maybe even now, he was ensconced in a Nez Perce tipi, enjoying a warm fire and admiring a whole herd of spotted mounts.

If Joel were a praying man, he'd say a prayer for that to be true. But he'd never liked the religion the government foisted on people back in Andalusia, and he'd not said a prayer since their ship sailed away from the Spanish coast.

He'd been tempted to once or twice as he watched Caleb and Beaver Tail and Susanna. Their faith seemed nothing like the demanding religion he'd witnessed in Spain, especially during the days of the Inquisition. More than once he'd heard his friends talk about the love of their God. They made Him sound like He knew each of them individually and...well, personally.

It didn't make sense. And Joel had not worked up the courage to ask more about Him.

He pulled the saddle from the gelding's back and hoisted it over one of his shoulders, then the pack over his other. He dropped them both with the rest of the supplies and spread an oilskin over everything. This way, they wouldn't have to scramble if a sudden rain or snow began in the night.

A glance toward Meksem showed she'd finished unsaddling their mounts and was stroking one of the horses. She looked softer doing that, more like a woman than a fierce warrior. She'd probably plunge a knife in him for the thought.

He started to call for her to place her things under the oilskin with the rest but caught himself before speaking. She wouldn't understand his English.

So he waved to catch her attention, pointed to the pile of saddles and packs beside her horse, then lifted the oilskin and motioned to a corner where she could place her things. He would do it for her, but she might think he was trying to steal them.

When she nodded her understanding, he made a final pass down the tie line, stroking muzzles and checking each horse's rope as he went. All seemed secure.

At last, he could turn himself toward the warmth of the campfire someone had managed to coax to life, and the food he could already smell. Two years before, he'd never have thought he could be so grateful for a bit of warmth and something to soften the gnawing in his belly.

And if he had to be honest with himself, the woman who raised her intriguing dark gaze to meet his as he approached might be the strongest enticement of all. Maybe with some time spent around the campfire, he could learn her story.

CHAPTER 5

*E*lan had never experienced the sense of kinship these four men and one woman seemed to share. They couldn't be related, as each seemed to be from a different tribe of people. A different country, they called it.

But their easy manner of talking, the give and take of thoughts and jesting, the familiar grins—everything bespoke a heart-deep respect she'd not often seen. She hadn't been able to understand much they said, but their tones and expressions spoke more clearly than words.

Of course, more than respect existed between Susanna and Beaver Tail. Once the evening chores were complete, the woman had snuggled in next to her brave, and every so often, they shared a look that made Elan's chest hurt.

The ache was more for what would never be than what had once been. She and Chuslum might have reached that point in time. The pleasant respect between them may have deepened into the obvious love these two shared.

But now, she would never know.

The dark-haired man, French, spoke something her weary mind couldn't follow, then Joel leaned forward to answer. He paused before any words came out, then glanced her way and attempted to sign his response as he spoke. *My brother had a horse like the one he speaks of.* He nodded toward French.

Between the gestures and the few American words she picked out, she understood everything. Strange how the cadence of his voice was easier to understand than that of the others.

Joel's brow wrinkled in thought, then he looked to Beaver Tail and must have asked how to make a certain sign. The blazing campfire between them hid the motion of the brave's hands, but then Joel turned to her with his mouth tipped in a sideways grin. Again, he spoke in the white man's tongue while he made the signs. *His horse would not let another ride it unless my brother was near.*

Again Joel looked to Beaver Tail and spoke a question. This time the man responded in her own tongue. "Calm."

Joel rolled the word through his mouth, then nodded and used the word before switching to signs. *With my brother.* Then he made a motion with his hands of a horse jumping in a wild buck and grinned at her as he finished the sentence in the language of sign. *When not with my brother.*

She couldn't help a smile at the man. His story held its own slight humor, but as he struggled to remember and form signs to tell his account—a simple tale he could have easily left them out of—his face lost the fierce intensity he usually portrayed. Instead, his features shifted freely with each motion, as though he stopped forcing himself to be what he thought he *should* be.

The freedom made him come alive, and his energy ignited something in her own chest.

And the way he worked so hard to make sure she and Meksem could understand… Elan had never been treated with so much respect by a man.

Meksem probably wouldn't understand. She'd proven herself an equal among the warriors in their village and was respected as one of them. But Elan had only wanted to be the center of her little family. The best mother possible to Alikkees and a capable wife to Chuslum, keeping a lodge he looked forward to coming home to.

No matter how hard she'd worked at that, she'd never been given so much deference as Joel now offered. Part of her hesitated to enjoy the attention. The men should be able to talk freely without worrying about her or going to extra work to make sure she and Meksem could be part of the discussion.

She settled a little deeper into her furs, letting herself be swallowed more fully in the shadows. Mayhap if she stayed quiet, Joel would turn his attention back to his friends. She could be content to watch from the fringes.

～

*J*oel scanned the cliff ahead as he rode the next morning, studying the distant trail that wound around the peak in a spiral. Surely Meksem wouldn't lead them along that tiny strip that barely jutted off the side of the cliff. Could an animal really find footing on that almost vertical slope?

As if to mock him, a head popped up at one end of the trail, gradually growing into a small body.

"Is that a mountain goat?" Susanna voice sounded from where she rode just behind his packhorse.

He squinted. "The head doesn't look quite right. Look how long those horns curl."

"Bighorn sheep." Her voice grew with excitement. "I remember Lewis and Clark writing of them in their journals."

Ahead of him, Elan turned in her saddle. Each time she looked his way, her eyes grabbed him anew, pulling him with a draw he couldn't quite explain.

He forced his focus away from her face and pointed toward the distant animals. "Bighorn sheep."

She glanced to where he motioned, then looked back at him with a half-smile showing in her eyes. *"Tnúun."*

He sat straighter and replayed the word in his mind to pick out all the sounds. His tongue rolled through the syllables, then he spoke them aloud. "Tnúun."

Maybe his accent wasn't as fluent as hers, but from the surprised lift of her brows, he must not have been too far off.

The fur covered her mouth, but her smile glimmered in her eyes.

He forced his focus back on the sheep, which had turned into a herd of six traipsing along the path. He turned his head enough so his voice would carry to the others behind him. "Do we need meat?"

"We have enough for four or five more days." Caleb's voice drifted up from the rear of their group.

Meksem looked back at them from her place in the lead, confusion marking her face. Beaver Tail spoke a string of words that must have been in her language, for she answered in the same tongue. Try as he did, Joel couldn't make out a single word. Especially not with them both speaking so quickly.

Beaver moved his horse out of line as he pulled his rifle from its scabbard.

"What did she say?" Joel reached for his own gun.

"Little animals in mountains. Need hunt when we see them." Elan's voice pulled his focus her direction.

He nodded. Meksem seemed a capable guide and woodsman but not as comfortable with English as Elan.

Within less than a minute, Beaver Tail had brought down one of the sheep and rode ahead to dress the meat. The rest of them kept at the pace Meksem had set throughout the morning. In another quarter hour or so, they'd catch up with him, but knowing Beaver Tail, he'd have everything done by then and be ready to tie the carcass on his packhorse.

As they dipped through the narrow valley between the two cliffs, preparing to climb up to where the bighorn had been, a rustling to their left snagged Joel's attention. His hand went for his rifle as a movement shifted between the trees.

The women riding just ahead of him halted their horses as he did his own. Whatever approached was bigger than a single animal. A group...of men?

He nudged his gelding forward so his mount shielded Elan and Meksem. Caleb and French would do the same for Susanna.

It shouldn't have surprised him when Meksem reined her horse up beside his. Clearly, she considered herself one of the protectors.

As the oncoming group neared, he could make out fur-skin-draped men atop horses, and some of the mounts wore the same spots as the two Elan and Meksem rode.

His blood surged as a new thought penetrated. Could Adam be in this group?

His mount must have felt his anticipation, for he had to hold the gelding back while they waited for the strangers to near.

When they grew close enough to make out faces, he scanned each of the half dozen men—all tawny skinned and without any familiar features.

His heart dropped like a stone in his gut. For a long moment, he couldn't quite push the disappointment aside.

But he had to. They still needed to know if these men were friend or foe, and maybe they'd have news of Adam.

The group stopped two horse lengths away, and Joel studied each face again to see which man considered himself the leader. Meksem must have assumed his pause meant he wanted her to take the lead, for she straightened and spoke a string of sounds.

The only word he picked out from her statement was

Pikunin, which he was pretty sure was the name of one of the Nez Perce bands.

One of the two men riding in the lead answered her, his round face bobbing as he spoke. Meksem responded, and Joel shifted his gaze between her and the strangers. None of them looked angry or threatening.

He couldn't find a sign of friendship either, so these must not be members of their same village. How many towns did the Nez Perce occupy? Were there only a few families in each camp and multiple camps spread across the land they covered? Or maybe the tribe lived only in large settlements. He should have asked Beaver for more details of the people they were traveling so far to locate.

Conversation bounced back and forth between Meksem and the brave, and Joel's frustration grew more with each volley. The man pointed back the way the braves had come as he spoke.

Should Joel interrupt and ask Meksem what was being said? Would she think to ask about Adam? Surely she would, since that was the entire reason they were trekking through these mountains in the peak of winter. But it would be just like a woman to get lost in small talk.

Before he could motion to her, Elan guided her horse up on his other side, sandwiching him between the two women. He sent her a quick raised-brow look.

"They are Nimiipuu like us. Meksem asks about your brother."

A bit of the knot in his chest eased. "Good." At least she wasn't missing the opportunity.

Finally, the conversation seemed to end. The braves turned to continue on the path Joel had just traveled. Neither Elan nor Meksem moved as the strangers rode away, and it took everything in him to keep from asking his questions before the men were out of hearing range.

37

At last, Elan turned to him. Her eyes held a glimmer that looked almost like excitement. "See white man."

Joy surged through him. "They've seen Adam? When?"

She held up two fingers, then made the motion for a day.

"Two days ago? Where?"

The others had gathered around them now, and Susanna piped up. "Was Adam still with the Shoshone?"

Elan nodded. "Riding to Kannah village."

He flipped back through his memory for any time Beaver Tail had used that word. Wasn't the Kannah another of the Nez Perce bands?

She must have read his mind, for she pointed to herself, then Meksem. "Pikunin band." Then to the direction the warriors had departed. "Travel to Kannah camp, beside river white men call Clearwater."

The hope inside him surged. Would Meksem be able to lead them directly to the Kannah people? How far were they from the village where Elan lived?

Elan raised her flat palm and pointed to the tip of her middle finger. "Pikunin camp." Then to the center of her palm. "Kannah camp." Then she raised her head and nodded the direction the men had approached from. "We go there." She was good at reading his mind. Very good.

Joel sent a glance toward where Beaver Tail would be working the sheep carcass. They wouldn't be climbing that mountain now, which meant they'd need to call him back.

But before Joel could act on that, a hand touched his arm. Elan had moved her horse nearer him, and the concern in her gaze tightened the knot in his belly. Had the men said something more?

"White man sick."

A knife pierced his gut, deepening the pain coiling there. "Sick how?" An image flashed through his mind of Adam, pale and bent over his horse, barely able to hold on. Those braves had seen him two days ago, only half the time it would take to get out of these mountains. That must mean Adam still traveled in this glacial cold that bit through bone and marrow, tormenting even a man in good health.

How much more miserable must this bitter cold make Adam feel?

She shook her head, something like pity darkening her expressive eyes. She shrugged. "No say."

So now his imagination had free rein to conjure every possible form of sickness. Adam's condition must be bad for these Indians to recognize it in passing. Were any of his companions able to care for him? Did they have medicine to help relieve his symptoms?

Elan's hand pressed his arm again, pulling him back from the dark churning of his thoughts. She didn't speak, but her eyes pierced him, burning with a fierce determination that tried to spark hope in the turmoil of his mind.

"We find." She squeezed his arm, nurturing the spark into a tiny flame.

He inhaled an icy breath, then exhaled. *Yes, they would find Adam. They had to.*

He couldn't let his last living relative—the brother he'd spent his life cleaning up after thanks to one scrape after another—die in this remote mountain wilderness.

CHAPTER 6

*E*lan glanced at Susanna as she sliced the last of the meat from the bighorn sheep. She liked this woman, and they were finally developing an easy way of working together. Susanna didn't seem to know any of Elan's tongue, and the signs she knew had little to do with cooking, but Elan had been picking up more of the white man's words all day. Mostly, she and Susanna were able to communicate with gestures.

And smiles.

Even now Susanna smiled her thanks as Elan pushed the bark piled with meat strips toward her. Susanna's own hands were red with the animal's juices, but she pointed an elbow toward the metal pot, then nodded to a blank patch of snow.

Not hard to decipher her meaning.

Elan took up the pot and moved outside the ring of firelight to where the snow would be purest. First, she scooped the dish full of icy crystals, filling the pot full so there would be enough water once the snow melted. Then she plunged her own hands in the frigid white to clean the blood and grease from them.

She clenched her teeth to keep from cringing at the stinging cold on hands she'd thought were too numb to feel.

A movement in the shadows stilled her, and she peered deeper as every nerve inside her tensed. Even as she strained to see and hear and smell, she eased her hands around the pot's wooden handles and tucked her legs underneath her to spring away.

The blood from the meat might have drawn any number of predators. She hadn't heard of many mountain cats in this area, but they did sometimes venture here when they couldn't find game farther north.

A tiny whine broke through the stillness. Then a shadow shifted, stepping forward, separating from the darkness. A low form, like a wolf, but smaller.

She clutched the pot harder. She should run, but something held her still. Crouched low like this, a wolf might think her easy prey, especially if he already smelled the blood of a wounded animal.

Another whine drifted through the darkness, and the animal crept forward. Not like an attacking predator but like a hungry dog begging for a scrap of food.

She eased out a slow breath so the white cloud didn't frighten the creature. "Here, little one." Little by little, she loosened her grip with one hand and extended her fingers toward the mutt. The form of a dog was certain now, and it crouched lower as it crept toward her, as though it feared being struck at any moment.

Her heart pinched at the pitiful form. "I won't hurt you." She crooned the words in the voice she'd used to soothe Alikkees when a night terror awoke her.

The animal neared enough to sniff her fingers, then a tiny red tongue peeked out to lick her. Its warmth sent a sweet sensation all the way up her arm to curl in her chest. She didn't dare move.

"If you'll stay here, I'll get some food for you." She kept her voice soft and gentle, barely louder than a whisper.

The dog didn't flinch, just eyed her with dark eyes reflecting moonlight. Its fur, the color of tree bark, had helped it hide among the trunks and shadows, but now stood out distinctly against the snow.

She eased her hand away, then crept backward, not rising until she'd moved far enough away her height wouldn't present a threat.

After stepping into the ring of firelight, she settled the pot among the coals beside the leaping flame. "A dog found our camp. He's friendly and looks hungry and cold." She turned to find a bone covered in scraps of flesh the dog would enjoy.

Susanna looked up at her with questions in her eyes, and only then did Elan realize she'd spoken in her own tongue. She bit back a sigh. How wonderful it would be if they could all just understand each other.

Elan thought through what she'd said and how she could show her words in gestures, but before she could form any ideas, Beaver Tail spoke up, translating for his wife.

He really did seem to be a decent sort. Meksem still held fast to her suspicions, but Elan had only seen kindness and watchfulness from him, nothing that would hint at a bad nature. And love cloaked his every interaction with his wife. Something every woman would be grateful for.

When he finished speaking, he turned to Elan. "You think he's not dangerous?"

She scooped up what was left of a hip bone. "He is too cold and hungry to mean harm."

When she stepped into the darkness again, part of her expected the animal to have run away, back into the shadows where fear overcame hunger and gradually stole the life from it.

But the dog sat where she'd left it.

"Here, little one." She bent low and held out the bone as she approached.

The dog jumped to its feet and looked as though it might run away at any moment, but it stayed planted. Wise animal.

When she extended the bone to its nose, the dog shivered with anticipation. The animal licked the greasy end, then sent a tentative glance her way before closing its mouth around the meat.

She released the bone. "There now. If you come near the fire, there's more of that. Warmth, too." The animal's thick hair had clumps of snow matted around its feet. Weather like this was too hard on a dog. Her heart ached as the lean creature tore into the meat with desperation.

Reaching out slowly, she eased forward another step until she could lower her hand to stroke the dog's head. If the pup growled, she'd jerk her hand back. But it didn't.

She ran her fingers over the soft fur, rubbing the spot behind an ear that dogs seemed to love. The animal leaned into her touch. It had clearly been someone's dog. Mayhap even a beloved friend.

"Come, little one. Let's take you to the fire." She stroked its head once more, then pulled back and patted her leg. "Come."

The dog stood, bone in its mouth, and stepped toward her. Her chest eased in relief.

She walked toward the camp, and each time she tapped her leg and said, "Come," the dog took a few more steps forward.

When she reached the edge of firelight, the creature slowed, crouching as though it would dart away at the smallest threat.

"Here." Susanna handed her another small bone with meat still attached.

Elan held out the treat and called the dog again.

It crept forward, stepping past the mound of snow they'd cleared away to lay the fire.

"Good, little one." She laid the second bone on the ground and waited as the dog finally chose sustenance over fear.

While she and Susanna finished cooking the food, the dog

sat with its two bones, working its jaw until nothing remained except faint markings in the snow. It kept a wary eye on the others traipsing back and forth from the horses to the fire, going about the night's responsibilities.

She couldn't help but watch Joel's reaction the first time he stepped into the ring of firelight. He carried two packs toward the stack tucked against the stone wall on one side of their camp, but he paused mid-stride when he saw the dog.

"Hey." He darted a glance to Elan, and she met his look with a smile that would tell him all was well. The animal wasn't a threat.

He finished carrying the packs to their place, then moved toward the dog, using slow tentative steps as he bent low and held out a friendly hand.

The dog watched him but didn't stop gnawing on its bone. Not even when Joel lowered his gloved hand to stroke its head. His hands weren't over-large. Not like her husband's had been, but they fit Joel's well-proportioned features. He was average height, but every part of him seemed fit together seamlessly, letting him move with a lithe grace and intense passion that stirred something in her. As though he had the ability to love deeply, if only he could release the reserve that restrained him.

She hadn't expected him to linger with the dog. In truth, she hadn't thought he'd take the time to give the animal any notice at all, not as cold and weary as they all were.

But he did. After stroking the dog's head a few times, Joel lowered to a crouch and scratched the animal's ears, working his hands down its back. He murmured something to it, but with his voice so low, she couldn't make out the foreign words.

The dog leaned into his touch, almost turning over on its back as Joel scratched and rubbed. Its former owner must have been a man. One who showed kindness, at least to his animals. Some of The People might think such a man weak, but she'd always considered kindness and tenderness a mark of strength in any person, male or female.

Now, watching Joel with the dog lodged a ball of emotion in her throat. She turned away, back to the camas bread she'd been kneading.

She couldn't let herself grow attached to this man. After he found his brother, he'd be gone from her life forever. And she couldn't handle losing another person she loved.

She couldn't let herself be so vulnerable.

~

*A*s they rode through rocky terrain the next day, Elan held tight to the pup perched across the front of her saddle. Maybe she should have tried to get the dog back to the man who'd first laid claim to him. The stranger had clearly been kind to the animal, or the dog wouldn't have been so willing to trust strangers. Maybe the man had held affection for the sweet bundle of warmth that now lay across her lap as she rode.

Perhaps the dog had belonged to one of those braves they'd met early yesterday, but she'd probably never know. After the pup had snuggled against her leg all night, warming her both inside and out, there was no way she would turn back to seek out the group.

Besides, with the new urgency marking Joel's features, driving his every action, he likely wouldn't allow the group to turn back. And separating from the others to strike out on her own may well have been a death sentence in these mountains. She had to stay alive to help find Joel's brother.

There was no other choice, she'd have to keep her sweet friend. She stroked the dog's head, and he looked at her with dark, trusting eyes. Her heart swelled even more. Maybe developing so much affection for the dog wasn't wise, but she couldn't help that now.

She'd simply have to make sure she kept him safe.

By the time they stopped at midday, snow had begun to fall in a steady flow. Gentle flakes for now, without the wind that had gusted last time. She huddled deeper in her furs, allowing only a single opening for her eyes. The dog snuggled close, completely covered by her bearskin cloak.

None of them spoke as they pressed on, riding uphill through woods as they curved around the base of a mountain.

At last, Meksem signaled for the group to halt, then turned her horse to face them. "We leave the trees soon to climb a steep mountain. We can wait here until the snow stops or press on. The danger to keep going with snow falling will be great."

Beaver Tail spoke the moment she stopped, interpreting for the others. Elan strained to catch each of his words. Now that she focused on understanding the white man's tongue—English, Susanna called it—she was picking up more and more each day. But although hearing was coming quickly, forming words on her own still proved a challenge.

By the end of this journey, she might be able to carry on a conversation. At least a short one. Maybe with Joel.

Her gaze slid to him, as it had every other heartbeat all day. It didn't help that he rode just in front of her, giving her a constant view of his strong outline, always at the ready. Always searching.

Now, his face bore hard determination. None of them need wonder whether he thought they should wait out the storm or push through.

For a long moment, only the stomp of Susanna's horse sounded amid the falling snow. Each of them looked to the mountain peak showing through the trees, the rocky face their horses would need to climb in the falling ice crystals. For her part, she wouldn't mind chancing the journey, but the others shouldn't risk such danger, nor their mounts. Nor the sweet pup snuggled against her.

Beaver Tail broke the silence first. "I think we should wait. It's too dangerous with the fresh snow." His glance moved to Susanna, and even his stoic warrior face didn't disguise the concern in his eyes.

"We'll lose half a day, maybe more." Joel's voice held enough tension to melt the falling snow.

"We'll lose our lives if we take foolish risks. Then how will we find Adam?" Beaver didn't sound angry, just the voice of reason.

Joel looked back at the mountain. "I'll ride on ahead. You can catch up with me as you're able."

"No." The word slipped out before Elan even thought about speaking. She struggled for the right words in his language to explain herself. "Stay together. Too much danger."

He met her eyes, his gaze dark and almost desperate. She understood his fear, remembered that same panic. If only she could take away his distress, replace it with a measure of peace.

But she had none of it herself. She couldn't give him what he needed.

"Maybe we can start up, then stop if the going gets too treacherous." Joel turned his focus to the others, looking from one to the next as if taking their measure. Or maybe pleading. His dark eyes certainly made *her* want to give in.

"A vote then." Caleb straightened. "All who agree to keep riding until the trail gets too dangerous, say aye."

She wasn't sure what *aye* meant, but she wanted to keep going, so she said the word, along with French, Joel, and Meksem.

"Looks like that's our plan." Caleb nodded. "We should take a moment to pray for God's protection."

She'd not spent much time around Caleb, mostly because his knowledge of sign language seemed to be the least of any of them. And also because his massive frame reminded her a little of Chuslum, and being near him sent a pang through her chest.

But his words grabbed hold of her. Throughout her life, she'd heard of the white man's God and the book that held His words. Her people had told stories of Him for many generations, but they'd not learned more until the white explorers came to visit a few years before she was born. Many of The People wanted to learn more of Him because of the great wealth He gave white men.

But that wasn't what had always drawn her.

From the first time she heard the stories, something had resonated in her heart. A God who created His people, then didn't leave them to fend for themselves but walked beside them, guiding and helping them. Every time she thought of it, an intense longing stirred deep inside her.

Maybe that showed the weakness in her spirit—the fact that she didn't want to be her own person. The fact that she wanted Someone greater to lean on.

Perhaps she *was* weak. Maybe if she knew who she wanted to be, she wouldn't need a greater strength. But the woman she'd thought she was had died with her daughter, leaving only the shell of a person behind.

Caleb was speaking again, and she forced the thoughts away so she could focus on his words. His head was bowed, as were the heads of the others in their party.

"Lead us on the safe path, Lord. Guide our animals and bring us safely to the other side. Take us to Adam and keep him healthy. In Christ's name, Amen." His voice held so much warmth throughout, it was as though he was speaking with a friend. A very good friend.

Everyone looked up, and, as she'd expected, Joel turned toward the mountain barely visible now through the thick falling snow. "Let's ride."

CHAPTER 7

*W*as he leading these people to their deaths?

Joel tightened his legs around his gelding as the horse lunged up the slick, rocky incline. For the first time in years, he wished he had someone to turn to. Someone stronger and greater than himself to give over this heavy load of responsibility.

The pressure was becoming too much.

If only Caleb's God could be as real as the man made Him sound. *Guide our animals and bring us safely to the other side. Take us to Adam and keep him healthy.* Caleb's words replayed over and over through Joel's mind. That was exactly what he wanted with everything in him.

If You're really there, get us over this mountain without anyone dying. Don't let me hurt these innocent people. And keep my brother alive. Let me find him. All that seemed too much to ask a God Joel hadn't ever allowed himself to truly acknowledge as real, not in his heart. But the mountain of need rising before him was piling higher with every step. The stakes were too great.

Help us. Please.

Behind him, the sound of rocks tumbling grabbed his focus.

He glanced back, the incline so steep he had to peer under his elbow. The line of horses still trudged upward, none having fallen.

He raised his gaze back ahead of him as his mount surged up onto a boulder. The gelding's back hooves slipped on the stone as they struggled for grip. He gave the animal its head, leaning forward to help it balance on the perch. Behind him, his packhorse strained against the tether rope he'd lengthened for travel up this peak. Maybe they should have left the three packhorses behind. But that would mean slow starvation for the animals and loss of supplies for the people. Would that be worse than the possibility of tumbling head over heels down the side of a rocky mountain?

Maybe he should have insisted he go on alone. *Yes.* This was madness, bringing all these people over this treacherous slope. The time had come for him to stop being selfish and make the best decision for the others.

When his gelding finally planted all four hooves on the boulder's surface, Joel reined the animal to a stop. The group behind him had already paused when his horse slipped, and they now looked at him with expectant faces.

"I'm going on ahead. You all need to turn back. Take my pack horse. There's no sense risking him too." He'd just need to move a few supplies to his saddlebags. Namely, food.

Expectancy shifted into worry on most of the faces that stared back at him.

"We said we're all goin' together, Joel. That means we're stickin' together." Caleb spoke first, one of those who hadn't voted to proceed in the snow in the first place. But his tone sounded determined now.

It didn't matter, Joel was just as determined. Even more so. He'd not kill his friends in the process of finding Adam.

His gaze slid to Elan. Yes, she'd become a friend too. He wished he could talk with her—truly talk, without the frustrations of language between them. But he'd known from that first time he saw her as she walked out of the cave, that first time he'd been captured by her fathomless gaze, that she was a friend. Someone he'd been destined to meet.

Now, he had to let her go.

He looked down at the stone his horse stood on. There'd be just enough room for him to stand, too, if he was careful. Sliding down between his horse and the cliff's side, he gripped the saddle until his feet touched stone.

"Joel, we're going with you. Get back on and ride." Susanna's tone sounded like that of a pesky big sister.

He'd never had a sister, but he'd had a pesky older brother, and he'd learned more than one way around that bossiness. Of course, Joel refusing to comply was why Adam had taken off by himself in the first place, determined to find the famous Palouse horses and obtain one for himself. If only Joel had agreed to go along. They'd always done everything together. Instead, Adam had sneaked off on his own.

He pushed the thoughts aside, along with the echo of Susanna's words that lingered in the snowy air. Dropping to his haunches, he slid down the boulder's side to the lower level where his packhorse waited, then moved to the satchel containing some of their food. "I'll just take enough to see me a couple days."

He glanced over at Meksem. "After this mountain, travel southwest?" He used his hands to help explain his question.

Her brows lowered in a frown, and her mouth puckered like she'd eaten an unripe cherry—more expression than her face usually offered. He made the motions again, trying to prompt some kind of response from her. She'd been the one leading them, the only one who knew the way.

Finally, she sent a glance to Elan, then looked at him again and shook her head. "All go." Her accent was so thick, his cold mind took a moment to interpret the words.

Then he had to fight down a growl. Even this woman, who'd shown so little warmth, was going to thwart him.

He turned his attention toward the full group. "I can't put you all at risk like this. I understand it's foolhardy to climb this mountain in any weather, but especially with so much ice and snow. But I have to get to my brother. I'll go on ahead. If you want to wait until the terrain is safer, come then. If not, I understand. I hope to see you again someday." The last words clogged in his throat, but he pushed them out. This wasn't the time to get sentimental.

As much as these people had come to mean to him, especially the men he'd come to love like brothers, his *real* brother needed him. Maybe Adam's life depended on Joel reaching him. He had to help. He had to.

"We're all going, Joel. You don't get to decide for us." French spoke up now, his voice ringing from the back of the group. "Climb back on your horse and ride before we freeze to death on the side of this hill."

Guns and saddles, if these weren't the most stubborn people he'd ever faced off with. If they wanted to kill themselves, apparently he couldn't stop them.

He bit down his frustration but didn't bother trying to hide his glare. "I can't protect you. Each of you needs to choose for yourself."

He didn't let himself watch their reactions, just climbed back up on the boulder and slid between his horse and the rock. The old boy had been remarkably patient—all the horses had—but getting back up on him now would be a trick. Good thing he'd practiced mounting the animal from both sides.

Without daring to breathe, Joel placed his foot in the stirrup and eased himself up, staying close and low on the horse so he didn't throw its balance away from the cliff and send them both tumbling to their death.

At last, he settled in the saddle with both feet in the stirrups.

He let out a long breath as he straightened and grasped the tether line again.

He didn't let himself stop to think about what would come next, just gave his packhorse a tug and signaled his mount forward.

He may not have the chance to breathe again until they descended the other side of this mountain.

~

*T*his helplessness was almost as bad as the grief she'd carried since summer. Elan leaned farther back in her saddle, loosening her legs around her mount to give the animal freedom to maneuver the steep downhill grade. Her people were wise to use saddles like the white men instead of riding bareback as some tribes did. The ups and downs of the mountains would be hard to traverse without stirrups to brace against.

At least they'd made it to the top of the peak without incident, and now that they'd descended halfway down the far side, the snow was beginning to ebb. Of course, the fresh layer of icy crystals covering the rocks only made the route more slippery.

Her gaze shifted up to Joel, two horses ahead at the front of their group. The knot in her belly coiled tighter as his head bobbed. This entire way down the mountain, her breath had hitched every time his head dropped low while his horse maneuvered down another layer of rock. Was this the time the animal would stumble, throwing them both forward, rolling them down the mountain to strike head and body against jagged stone? Surely neither man nor beast could survive such a fall.

Again, the helplessness pressed down on her shoulders, smothering her with the weight of her fears. Even if she'd not let her heart grow tender toward him, she would worry over his safety, just as she did for all the people in this unlikely group.

But the fact had become achingly clear as they'd traversed this dangerous cliff—she'd allowed this man to seep into her heart, no matter that they'd barely had a decent conversation. She'd watched his steadfastness, the kindness he tried to mask with that layer of intensity. She'd seen the way he was willing to give his very life to help his brother. Even the sweet pup riding in her lap approved of him, a favor the dog hadn't even offered to Meksem yet. Animals often had a keen sense about people, at least about the untrustworthy ones.

Joel had won over both her and the dog. If something happened to him now... She couldn't stand another round of grief. Maybe he wasn't as dear to her as little Alikkees had been, nor Chuslum, even though she and her husband had not had a chance to grow close. But the thought of losing Joel pierced her heart with a feeling too much like that other grief.

A grunt from ahead jerked her attention forward just as Joel's head bobbed low. Her heart clutched as she leaned sideways to see around Meksem.

The sight before her surged fear through her chest.

Joel's horse lost its footing and tumbled forward. A scream tore from her throat as the world around her seemed to slow.

His horse landed on its side. Then rolled. Joel must have let go of his pack animal, but for some reason he didn't push away from his own mount. Maybe his limbs were as leaden with fear as her own were.

The first roll catapulted them into another. Then another as the two of them tumbled down the rocky slope.

"No!" Meksem's yell ripped Elan from the shock that froze her, jerking her into action.

She leaped from her horse, laid the dog on the ground, and charged toward Joel. Voices clamored behind her as she pushed past her friend's mount, then around the pack gelding.

With nothing else concealing her vision, she couldn't take

her gaze from Joel's black gelding, still rolling but slower now, nearing the base of the mountain where the slope evened.

Joel. She could barely tell if that was him, covered in snow, still pressed on his horse's back.

She didn't stop to stare, just flew as fast as she dared, running and sliding past snow-covered boulders, over stones jutting out through the skid marks left by the falling horse.

Fear surged with every beat of her heart. Would Joel be alive? Could anyone survive being crushed by the weight of a horse so many times? Had any of the stones struck his head? Broken bones? What would be left of him?

A lifetime passed before she reached him. She was running so fast, her body almost propelled her beyond the horse. Her legs scrambled to keep up with her momentum.

She finally sat hard in the snow to stop herself just before she would have plunged into the animal.

"Joel." She paused to take in the pair, to see if either he or the horse moved.

The animal raised its head, and a measure of relief slipped through her. "You're safe, boy." It worked one front leg forward, and realization that it might try to stand soon jolted her into action. She had to get Joel away from the animal.

He lay curled over the horse's back, not moving, covered in pressed snow. She reached out, part of her not wanting to touch him. Was he dead? *He couldn't be dead.*

Not Joel, too.

CHAPTER 8

*E*lan pulled her glove from her hand and pressed fingers to Joel's cheek. Still warm. How long would it take a lifeless body to cool in this frigid air?

The others had come now, gathering around, their fear thickening the air as they all watched for signs of life.

Joel's eyes flicked open, and she jerked her hand back. "Joel."

He lay still for a moment, only his eyelids shifting, as though he was thinking hard about something. Maybe trying to remember what had happened or wondering where he was.

The gelding shifted again, working its other front foot out of the snow.

"We need to get you away from your horse." She reached for Joel's shoulder.

At first, her hand resisted touching him. Maybe because of the many years of keeping to herself. Women didn't spend time around the warriors, and they certainly didn't touch them.

But Joel needed help. She had to act quickly, or he could be hurt worse when his horse tried to stand.

She reached for his leg and worked his foot out of the stirrup. The other leg was pressed under the horse's back, his boot probably still hooked in the stirrup there too.

Her action seemed to pull Joel from his stupor, for he shifted onto his back, his face scrunching into a groan.

Beaver Tail moved to the horse's head, holding it still so the animal didn't try to rise until Joel was free from the stirrups.

She positioned herself behind Joel and reached for his upper arms. "Need move him back."

Caleb nudged her aside. "Let me."

She obeyed, allowing him the heavy work while she made sure Joel's legs came free of the horse and saddle. Beaver Tail held the animal's reins and helped the gelding stand. She could hardly believe it could manage the feat, that no broken bones had been suffered in the fall. But the horse stood on all four hooves, head hanging low as it sucked in heaving breaths.

She turned her focus back to Joel, who seemed to have come back to life with the movement. He raised a hand to ward them off. "I'm all right. Just...let me up."

Turning on his side, he worked himself up to his elbow. Was he really not injured? How could that be possible? She'd seen him rolling with the horse, over and over down the mountainside. Being pressed down by the giant animal more times than she could count on all her fingers.

Joel stayed in that position, propped up on his elbow. Hard breaths raised his shoulders as he stared up at the horse. "He hurt?" He seemed to be struggling for air, but maybe that was to be expected after the animal pressed everything out of his chest.

Beaver Tail ran his hands down the horse's neck, around the belly, and over all four legs. "God protected him."

Joel worked himself up to a sitting position. Elan longed to help, especially when none of his friends stepped in to assist. But from the hard line of his jaw, she had the feeling Joel would shake away any offer. He was just stubborn enough not to want coddling.

As Joel sat with his legs bent, arms resting on his knees, Beaver moved to crouch in front of him. "And you? Anything broken?"

Joel gave a single shake of his head. "Nothing."

Beaver Tail nodded. "God protected you, too." He spoke the words with certainty, as though he had no doubt of their truth.

Slowly, Joel nodded. Then he winced, as though his head pained him. "You might be right."

He needed to rest. And some of the snow may have seeped through to his skin. He would freeze soon if he didn't get warm.

"We camp now." She turned to look around for a good spot. They were below the steepest part of the mountain now, and a small section of trees grew a little farther down.

She looked back at Joel. "Can you walk?" She pointed to the trees.

"Yes." He clamped his jaw tight and worked himself up to his knees.

She couldn't bear watching him struggle alone anymore. After pushing to her feet, she reached out and took his upper arm, helping him balance as he eased up to standing.

He gave her an unsteady look that he might have meant as a smile, but he didn't pull back. His head must be spinning. If he tried to walk on his own, he'd likely end up tumbling down the rest of the hill.

She slipped herself under his arm, draping his hand around her shoulders so he'd have support to help him balance. Again, he didn't pull back, just settled his arm around her shoulders in a way that felt almost protective. She was supposed to be the one helping him, but the warmth of his touch cloaked her with a security that soothed her all the way through. Together, they hobbled toward the trees while the rest of the group followed in caravan.

Joel limped heavily beside her at first, but the farther they walked, the more he stood upright. His arm never moved from her shoulders, though. If anything, his hold tightened, tucking her tighter against his side.

She didn't try to move away.

Just beyond the edge of the trees, he pulled to a stop and looked to the others. "Will this work?" Any other time, he would have simply stated this was the place they would camp, not asked the question. A fall like that would shake anyone's confidence.

As each person started into their usual night duties, Joel eased his arm away from her.

She studied his face. "You are not hurt?"

He reached up and scrubbed a hand over his face and let out a long breath. "No. Not hurt." Then his eyes met hers, softening with a tenderness that pulled at something deep inside her.

His mouth parted as though he were about to speak. But no words came out.

No words were needed. His eyes told her of his fears, both the fears for his brother that had driven him to crest the mountain with so much snow still falling, and the fear that he'd put them all at risk. They spoke an apology for the danger and for worrying her so, and even hinted at how shaken he still was after coming so near death.

She listened to everything his eyes told her, letting him see how much she understood. Letting him see he didn't have to bear the weight of his worries alone. She could help carry the load, be a strength when he needed help.

His throat worked, and his lips parted again. "Thank you." With a tiny nod, he turned away.

She exhaled a long, shaky breath, trying to pull her raw emotions back under control. At a time when she should be pulling away, guarding her heart from becoming too attached... what had she begun?

~

*J*oel had never hurt in so many places before. He hadn't even known it was possible to feel pain in some of the parts of his body that ached.

He'd not allowed himself to lie down until he did at least a little to help set up camp. Caleb had insisted Joel swap duties with him, leaving Joel to start the fire and gather enough wood for the night, an offer he didn't take long to accept. And he didn't complain too much when the others all brought loads of wood so he didn't have to go hunting for it. He wasn't sure he could have managed bending over to pick up logs.

His body felt weak as a babe's, his head still throbbed, and his vision still wobbled, especially when he moved too quickly.

Now, he finally let himself stretch out on his fur pallet and rest his aching eyes. Something warm and soft crept alongside him and settled in close. He would have smiled if the act didn't take so much effort. "Hey, boy." He shifted his hand to rest on the dog's back.

The mutt let out a long sigh and settled in closer, clearly exhausted. That made two of them.

The sounds of wood scraping metal drifted from where Elan and Susanna worked by the fire. The two seemed to get along well, although he rarely heard them talking. Susanna would occasionally comment on what she planned to do next, but Elan stayed so quiet.

Was it only the language barrier that kept her from speaking? He suspected she understood more English than she spoke, since she often seemed to know what they were all saying. So was there something more that kept her quiet?

Maybe something in her background? He didn't know much about Nez Perce customs and how women were treated. Maybe she'd been taught to stay in the background, giving preference to the men.

But that didn't make sense with what Beaver had said when

Joel asked his friend about the camas root she and Meksem ate. He'd said the women harvested the roots and used the plant as both food and trade goods, often becoming shrewd business-women with their own little empires.

So that left the question—did Elan stay quiet through lack of understanding of their language, or because she'd never been shown that her voice was worthy of being heard?

An idea slipped in, and he acted on the thought before he could talk himself out of it. "Elan?"

"Yes." Her voice sounded hesitant.

He didn't open his eyes to study her, as much as he'd like to watch her pretty form while she worked. But maybe not having him look on would make the conversation easier for her. "How do you say *family* in your language?"

Silence settled for a moment, then a word rolled off her tongue in a sweet, rhythmic melody. *"Init."* She had such a beau-tiful voice. Maybe one day he could find the opportunity to tell her—and the courage.

He replayed the word in his mind, working his tongue through the sounds. Then he tried it aloud. It wasn't the worst butchering he'd ever done. Not as bad as when he'd had to learn French as a lad.

He raised an eyelid to see if her face gave any reaction about how his effort had sounded.

A soft smile spread over her features, and, when she saw him looking, she nodded. "Good."

Susanna sent him a smile as well, then stood. "I promised to bring this food to Beaver. I'll be back shortly."

As the swish of her buckskins faded in the distance, he let his eyes drift shut again. Only the sound of Elan's work blended with the crackling of the fire. "Tell me of your init. You have brothers? Sisters? Parents?" Would she understand what he was asking?

Through the next few moments of silence, he had to force

himself to lay quietly, his only motion stroking the dog stretched out beside him. He wanted to watch her expressions, but staring might scare her away.

"One brother. Die as warrior. One sister. Marry Salish brave. Parents live."

His heart pressed. Did she feel alone as the only one left? Then another thought struck him, a force so hard it knocked the breath from his chest. Was she married also? Would she be wandering the mountains with only a female friend if she had her own brave somewhere? Surely not.

He opened his eyes to study her. She'd turned to stir something in the pot by the fire. With the flickering flames illuminating her beautiful face, he couldn't imagine that she'd gone so long, maybe into her early twenties, without every brave in the camp seeking her.

He forced words through his squeezing throat. "What of other family? A husband?" He should look away, but he couldn't make himself.

She didn't turn back to him as she answered. "Husband no more."

Husband no more. Three little words, spoken without emotion. Three words that carried so much meaning. So many questions. He'd died? For surely no man in his right mind would have given her up of his own accord. How long had they been together? Did she still love him? How long since he'd passed?

Then she did turn to Joel, and the wasteland in her gaze nearly strangled him. "Die from grizzly. Try to save our daughter."

His entire body went numb. From the barrenness in her gaze, the man hadn't been able to save their child. What pain Elan must have suffered. He couldn't imagine how much she must have hurt. Must still be hurting. Did one ever get over the loss of a child? Of a spouse?

Even with the little he'd seen of her nature, he had no doubt that even if hers hadn't been a love match, she would have cared for anyone she'd committed herself to. And then to lose them both in a single awful event.

He'd raised up onto one elbow without consciously thinking about the act. Part of him wanted to move closer to Elan and wrap his arms around her. To offer what small comfort he could.

But she'd already turned back to the pot. Probably trying to keep her emotions in check.

He had to say something. Somehow let her know he felt her pain as deeply as possible. That he wanted to be there for her. "Elan, I'm sorry."

She nodded. At least she understood the words. The delicate chords in her throat worked, and it looked like she might say something more.

After a moment, she did. "In the *táyam*. Time of hot weather." She raised her face, looking into the dark distance outside the firelight. "I mourn much. Need away from lodge."

He could well understand that. In part, that was why he and Adam had left Spain for the United States. After their parents' deaths in a wagon accident, Andalusia didn't feel like home any longer. Nothing was right anymore. "That's why you were crossing the mountains in winter."

She nodded, then dropped her focus back to the pot, stirring again.

He'd brought enough sadness from reminding her of her pain. Time he find something pleasant to speak of. "I'm glad we found you in that cave."

Her face softened, although he could only see one side as she looked down at her work. "The first good in many moons."

Warmth spread through him, and he eased back down to lay on the fur. He didn't close his eyes again, didn't conceal his watching as she worked with the food. Now that he knew a little of her past, the sadness he'd sensed before made sense.

But she also possessed a strength. How had he not seen it clearly before? This woman had been through fire, and even though she was still healing from the flame, she shone with the fine purity of the strongest diamond.

A gem so rare, he wasn't sure he would be able to part with her when this journey reached an end.

CHAPTER 9

"*H*ow in the great land of Jehovah can there be any snow left to fall?"

Elan had to smile at Caleb's amazed tone as more flakes drifted from the darkening sky above. The snow already piled almost to the horses' bellies, but it looked as if another deluge had just begun.

They'd been keeping a steady pace all day, weaving up and down mountains as they skirted the taller peaks. Now that night was beginning to fall, the animals must be exhausted, especially with the meager rations they'd been given these past days. Meksem has suggested that another day or two would take them to a plain where the horses could graze without so much snow to dig through for fodder.

"The horses need to rest. That overhang would be a good place to camp." Beaver Tail pointed to a stone wall ahead where something had worn the base of the rock away, leaving a covered cleft where the snow hadn't gathered as high. There wouldn't be much room to lay out bedrolls, but perhaps they could scoop away what little snow had blown under the shelter of the rock so their bedding wouldn't get as wet.

She couldn't remember the last time she'd been fully warm and dry.

As everyone set to work making camp and caring for the horses, there didn't seem as much for her to do as usual. She and Susanna had prepared extra food the night before, so most of it only needed reheating now.

French had gone to forage for wood and now dropped an armload on the bare ground they'd cleared for the fuel. "This is all I could find close by. I'll go farther back the way we came. I think I saw some fallen branches buried in snow beside the trail."

What he'd brought would only last half the night. They really needed at least as much again so they wouldn't freeze as the night winds blew through. Also, they'd need some to tie on Caleb's packhorse so they'd have dry wood to start tomorrow night's fire.

She pushed to her feet. "I go that way." She pointed the opposite direction. "Get wood."

He looked back at her, his gaze uncertain. "Be careful."

After nodding, she reached for her snowshoes and bent to tie the straps on. She had her knife and was as capable as anyone in these mountains. A nudge at her elbow brought a smile to warm her frozen face.

She ruffled the dog's head. "You want to come too?"

Trust glistened in his dark eyes, a dedication given so freely. How wonderful to not worry about the pain of losing those he gave his affection to. If only she could be as brave as this dog.

Rising, she started out, the pup bounding through the snow beside her. She had to go farther than she'd expected before finding enough wood, but finally she'd gathered a full armload and started back. When their camp came into view through the dusky light of almost-night, something unusual caught her attention.

Two braves sat by the fire, and neither looked like Beaver

Tail. Was this the right campsite, or had she missed a turn and come upon another group? No, that was definitely the same rock overhang.

She shifted closer to the mountainside, ducking low. The dog tucked himself against her as she studied the scene. There was Beaver Tail, standing like a guard with the rock at his back. Susanna knelt beside him as she worked over the fire. She could just make out Caleb and Joel, also kneeling near Susanna.

Fear eased out of Elan's chest. The two braves must be visitors.

As she made her way forward, the form of a third brave took shape, sitting near enough one of his friends that she'd thought the two shapes belonged to one man.

Joel and Beaver Tail both spotted her about the same time, and the others soon after. She studied the strangers as she stepped into the ring of firelight. Shoshone, from the looks of them. The knot in her middle coiled tighter.

Not all Shoshone were friendly.

The dog growled as he studied the new men. Not a ferocious sound, just a less-than-friendly greeting. "Easy." She murmured the word just loudly enough for the dog to hear, although some of the others might as well.

She dropped her load of wood on top of the rest, then moved to kneel between Susanna and Joel. The dog moved to Joel's other side, then sat upright, keeping a wary posture toward the strangers.

Susanna sent her a tight smile. "We have visitors. They were part of the group Adam was riding with."

Elan jerked her focus to Joel. His eyes had narrowed to dark circles, the muscles in his jaw stretched tight. She might not have noticed the differences before she came to know him, but now she could see the signs that his nerves were pulled tighter than a bowstring.

She shot a look at the braves but kept her voice quiet for Susanna and Joel. "Adam is better?"

"He's not better. They can't tell us what's wrong with him except that he's sick in his belly and has fever and sweats." The worry in Joel's voice pressed pain in her chest.

She studied his face to read what he wasn't saying. "How far?"

"They left him yesterday at midday."

Her heart leapt. They were catching up then. "Adam is alone now?"

He shook his head. "There are two braves still with him, taking him the rest of the way to the Kannah village."

A little of the tightness in her chest eased. "Good Adam not alone. We do well going to Kannah."

Joel gave a faint nod, but he looked as if he'd been holding his breath since the braves rode in. Would he want them all to ride out tonight?

"You want to leave now?" She wanted to reach out and touch his arm, something to take away his worry. But she didn't dare make such a move with all these people around. Warriors didn't like to be bothered in the thick of danger.

He eased out a breath so long, three heartbeats passed before he released the last of the anxious air. "The horses need rest. We'll leave at first light." Then he shot a glance to the braves who were talking quietly among themselves. He lowered his voice even more. "Something doesn't feel right about them."

Her shoulders tensed, and she slid a sideways look at the men so they wouldn't see her watching. "Shoshone usually not good."

Joel looked back at her, and for the first time since the braves appeared, his expression eased. A hint of a twinkle even flickered in his dark eyes. "I've always tried to judge a man according to his own actions, not what people or tribe he was born into. But there's something about them that doesn't sit right. Maybe the way they wouldn't give a straight answer until we pulled it out of them. They don't say a word to us unless we ask a direct question, and even then, they're not very friendly."

Part of her wanted to shrink back at Joel's reprimand, no matter how gently given. He was right, no one should be judged according to their tribe. But she'd been raised to be wary of Shoshone, even though her people were presently at peace with them. She'd heard so many stories around the lodge fires of the deceptive ways of the Shoshone. How they'd promised friendship, then stolen horses and run buffalo herds away from Nez Perce hunting parties.

Peace, the two tribes might share right now, but not trust.

But Joel was right. She had to be careful to judge these men on their own actions, not the feelings implanted in her youth.

French returned soon with another load of wood, and she helped him lay the wet logs out to dry near the fire's heat. Meksem finally slipped in from where she'd been lingering with the horses. The look she sent Elan made it clear she wasn't pleased with the presence of their visitors either. But with this being the only decent place to camp for a distance in both directions, it seemed cruel to send the men away.

Their presence kept the entire group quiet as they ate. Caleb tried to talk with the men, but they didn't know many white words, and he quickly gave up trying to sign.

Joel asked them about where their people lived and how they first met Adam, but the few words the braves answered seemed to be all they were willing to offer. They were returning to their people on the Great Plain, which was where they'd first met Adam when he approached their camp with a group of Mandan braves.

Snow began to fall again as they finished eating, quickly bringing an end to the night's conversation. Elan helped Susanna put away the foodstuffs while Meksem and Joel didn't hide the fact that they were standing guard.

With snow still drifting over them, Beaver Tail loaded more wood on the fire, then settled in next to his wife under the ledge. There was just enough room for the seven in their party to huddle mostly under the shelter and near enough the fire none of them would freeze. Sleeping upright wouldn't be the most comfortable option, but Elan likely wouldn't have slept well anyway with the presence of their Shoshone visitors.

That left the three braves to bed down on the opposite side of the flame, but not protected from falling snow. They didn't seem to mind, though, for they tucked under buffalo robes, covering everything except their eyes, which they closed as if they had nothing at all to worry over.

She sat sandwiched between Meksem and Joel, furs spread under them and buffalo robes covering. They would be warm enough, but she couldn't seem to focus on anything except the touch of Joel's shoulder against hers. His frame may not be as large as Chuslum's had been, but the solid touch of his broad shoulders proved his strength.

Laying her head back against the rock, she closed her eyes and forced herself to take in regular breaths. With Joel beside her, the strange braves no longer seemed the biggest threat to her peace. This man had the power to undo her. How had she let herself be so affected by him?

~

*J*oel kept his eyes closed as the warmth of steady breathing tickled his neck. Elan.

The slight weight of her head on his shoulder felt like a gift. Had she meant to trust him in her most vulnerable hours of sleep? Probably not, but he would treasure each moment.

Her breathing was as gentle as she was, and as steady too. Always there, never intrusive. The feathery soft brush of her hair on his cheek made him want to lean in. But would even that slight move wake her?

He'd settle for opening his eyes to watch her, even though he couldn't see much without turning his head. As he took in the way her slight form barely lifted the buffalo robe, a movement across the fire snagged his focus.

Maybe only a trick of the flame, but it looked as if one of the Shoshone had moved.

The dog saw it too, for he raised his head on Elan's other side, ears tuned toward the place across the fire where the braves slept. Like a dark spector, the buffalo skin rose up in a quick, lithe action, backing away from the fire to disappear into the night.

Joel tensed. He had to follow the man to see what he intended. If the man had only stepped out to make water, would he have taken his bedding with him? As cold as this night was… maybe. But Joel had to know for certain.

Elan must have felt his tension, for she lifted her head with a sleepy expression. He would love to stay and ease her from her groggy state slowly, but he had to follow the brave.

Slipping out of his place in the group, he reached for the knife at his waist and stepped around the fire, the dog trotting at his heels. A glance at where the other braves slept made the knot in his belly clench tight. All three were gone.

"Wake up, boys. There's trouble." He spoke loud enough to wake Beaver, who would make sure Caleb and French were alerted. The dog's yip helped, as the animal darted forward into the darkness.

Joel sprinted toward the place they'd tied the horses, a little farther around the mountain where a cliff would give the animals protection on one side. They'd moved most of their packs to the camp, but the saddles were near the horses, covered to keep them dry.

The soft nicker of a horse greeted him as he ran through the dark. Then the crunch of horse hooves in snow.

"Stop!" He could see figures now. The dark shape of a man at the head of Meksem's spotted mare. Of course the men would take the Palouse horses that had such a reputation for speed and endurance.

The man moved to the mare's side and vaulted up onto its back. Joel was close enough now to make a final lunge, closing the distance between them and grabbing the man's leg just as he wheeled the horse around.

CHAPTER 10

*J*oel clung to the buckskin legging with everything he had.

The brave kicked at him, trying to shed him like a loose boot, but Joel held tight. At last, he could feel the man slipping off the horse.

Men's shouts sounded around them, fierce barks from the dog, and a horse neighed frantically as one of the Indians loosed a high-pitched yell, almost like a war cry.

The brave Joel still held writhed in front of him like a mountain lion, spinning and leaping to one foot. The gleam of a blade shimmered in the scant moonlight, and Joel ducked as the knife caught in his coat's shoulder.

He reached for his own knife, leaving only one of his hands to hold the Indian's leg. The Shoshone seized the opportunity to wrest away.

The man screamed his own war cry as he sprinted toward the other horses.

Joel pushed to his feet and darted after him. Some of the animals had been cut loose, and two of them tore away from the others, bolting into the darkness with figures on their backs.

The dog dashed after them, his bark ferocious enough to draw blood with the sound alone.

"Get the other horses." French's voice cut through the night.

Joel veered to follow the command. He was pretty sure he'd seen a single Indian on each of the two horses, with the third climbing up behind his friend as the horse ran.

Within a few minutes, they'd gathered up all the horses. The women had come running at the same time as the men, and Susanna and Elan worked now to re-assemble the trampled tie rope. The dog came trotting back, his head low and tongue lolling.

"Looks like they got away with my pack horse and Caleb's mount. At least we have theirs to make up for them." Joel bit down his anger as he led the two Palouse mares and Susanna's riding horse toward the others. "Is anyone hurt?"

Worry festered in Susanna's tone as she said, "Beaver Tail has a knife wound."

"It's nothing." Her husband answered even before she finished the statement.

Joel glanced around the group again. "Anyone else?"

Elan met him by the rope and reached for her horse's lead. He let his gaze scan the length of her—no injuries that he could see—then honed in on her face. She searched his expression, and he tried to reassure her.

At least they were all safe, but he couldn't deny anger at his own stupidity. He never should have trusted those men.

He knew better than to ignore his instincts. And his instincts had screamed *danger* from the first moment none of the men would look him in the eye. He'd reasoned with himself that not all Indian tribes regarded eye contact as important in interactions with others. He'd told himself he'd want the chance to share a stranger's fire if he was exhausted and cold, with no protection from the elements for an hour's ride in any direction.

But he should have trusted his instincts.

After securing the horses, he moved to where Beaver Tail and French stood together. "Think they'll come back?" He met one man's gaze, then the other. Caleb stepped up to join them too, adding his solid presence in the group. These men had come to feel so much like brothers, there any time he needed them.

Not quite the way his own brother had always been.

More like the support Joel had always tried to be for Adam, even though Adam was the older. Without these three men, Joel may not have made it this far in his search. They were nearing their goal...only a day and a half apart.

Beaver Tail stared out into the darkness. "Maybe." The clench of his jaw rang clear in the sound of the word.

Joel glanced up to where the moon struggled to shine through the thick clouds. At least the snow had stopped. "We've slept half the night. Want to get moving?"

Quiet footsteps sounded behind him, and he shifted aside to let the women join their group. Was it only chance that brought Elan to stand by him? Her presence filled him with another layer of determination. He couldn't let her and Meksem lose their horses, or worse—their lives. The men had likely been targeting the two Palouse ponies.

"We go now." Meksem spoke with her usual forceful tone.

Joel glanced around the circle.

Caleb shrugged. "Fine with me."

Nods from the others eased the tension that had been building in his chest. "Let's break camp then."

Finally. They could take action.

~

*T*he horses' pace dragged slower and slower the next day. Even Elan's mare, who usually lasted longer even than Meksem's mount, plodded through the belly-high snow

75

with each step lagging more than the last. Her father had given her the spotted mare as a wedding gift, one of his finest stock, and she'd never been so grateful for the horse as on this journey.

Meksem finally called a halt as they reached the curve between two mountains at dusk. She motioned ahead of them to a sight that lifted a weight from Elan's shoulders. Far ahead stretched an open plain, its gently rolling hills covered in snow. In the distance, the dark swath of a river cut through the white.

A seed of something rose up in her chest. Maybe just a deep breath, but it felt like the first inhale after a long, long time of holding in spent air.

In truth, the fresh breath resurrected something inside her—a niggle of hope.

They'd made it through the mountains. Soon, they'd reach the Kannah camp perched in the crook of the river. And they'd find Adam.

She glanced sideways to catch Joel's expression.

He'd reined in his horse beside hers, and she'd never seen his focus so intense as the way he now stared out over the plain. Determination marked the set of his jaw, but the longing in his dark eyes shone through almost as fiercely.

Part of her wanted to reach out and touch his hand. To reassure him that they would find his brother, no matter what.

He must have felt her watching, for he turned and looked at her. She held his focus, letting her eyes say the words of her heart. The longing in his gaze didn't fade, but his eyes turned glassy, and red rimmed the outer white. The skin at the edges crinkled in acknowledgement of her silent message. A wordless *thank you.*

"We camp now. After sleep, we see Kannah camp when sun reach middle sky." Meksem turned her horse toward a cluster of three trees.

Elan braced herself for the work ahead. One final time, they'd set up camp, each person seeing to their duties. Joel had returned to his usual tasks and seemed to have mostly recovered from his tumble down the mountain. He showed no sign of aches—unless he thought no one was looking.

While she worked to clear a place for a campfire and light the tender they carried in one of the packs, Susanna readied food to be heated for the night's meal. Within minutes, French had gathered more than enough firewood from fallen branches to dry around the fire and use through the night, then carry with them the next day.

If fortune shone on them—or Caleb's God gave them clear passage—they wouldn't need dry firewood tomorrow. Surely the people would offer a lodge for them to share, along with seasoned fodder for the fire.

But they had to prepare for anything.

"That's the last of the corn for the horses." Caleb's voice drifted from where the men were stringing the tie line on the other side of the trees. "Good thing we'll be there tomorrow."

Meksem carried her pack and Elan's to the base of a tree where Joel was piling the others. Elan lifted her head from the tiny flame she'd kindled and sent her friend a weary smile. As exhausted as she was, smiling seemed easier now than before. Joel would finally find his brother. Tomorrow.

Her friend only nodded, then turned back to remove the horses' saddles. Elan refocused her attention on the blaze and laid another piece of bark at the edge of the flame. She blew a light wind to coax the wood to light.

A gunshot split the air. From nearby. Maybe right here in their camp.

Someone screamed. Or maybe that was her own throat as she ducked low. The dog barked, and she reached to grab him. He had to stay quiet.

Smoke clogged the air in the cluster of trees. A man yelled Joel's name. Another voice cried out in a painful moan.

"Joel!" Every part of her wanted to leap up and make sure he wasn't hurt, but she knew better than to run into flying bullets. Who was shooting at them? The braves who'd tried to steal the horses? She reached for the cooking knife tucked into her tall moccasin.

The gun smoke was clearing now, and she strained to see through the dim daylight to the figures moving around. Three forms—Caleb, Beaver Tail, and French—were bent over something on the ground.

Her chest clenched. *Joel.*

"Dear, God, no." Susanna's words were the last push Elan needed.

She released the dog, who darted toward the others, then she scrambled to her feet and bent low as she ran through the trees.

Joel lay on the ground. The others crowded around him. All except Meksem, who stood back against a tree, watching. French shifted sideways to allow Elan room, and she dropped to her knees beside Joel's head.

His eyes were open—those dark eyes that always drew her in—and he was breathing. She took a breath herself, maybe the first since she heard someone yell Joel's name.

"He's shot in the gut." Caleb's low voice drew her focus down to where Joel clutched a spot near the center of his belly.

His coat had been unbuttoned, and a red circle was spreading around the grip of his hands.

"Who?" She glanced up and scanned the area around them. The men weren't crouched, weren't attacking whoever did this to one of their own.

A horrible thought crept in, and she drew her gaze to their faces. First Beaver Tail's hard eyes, then the grim set of French's mouth, then the sorrow in Caleb's gaze.

No. Frantically, she spun to look for Meksem.

Her friend still stood beside the tree—motionless. Pale. The mask was stripped from her face, replaced by horror. She held a saddle clutched to her chest. Not hers or Elan's, but one of the men's. The base of the scabbard caught Elan's focus. The frayed edges of a black hole showed at the bottom, like a bullet had escaped through the leather.

No. In less than a breath, her focus flicked back up to Meksem's face, then to Caleb's. She couldn't miss the grim confirmation there.

No!

She pulled her gaze down to Joel. The red rimming his eyes sent a flash of memory through her. Another man's face, fierce pain carving every feature. Eyes red-rimmed and glassy. *No!* Her chest clenched tightly, and she nearly doubled over from the pain.

She would not watch Joel die as she had her husband and daughter. She had to *do* something.

Pushing Beaver Tail aside, she moved down to inspect the wound. "I need to see it." Little by little, she pried Joel's hands away from the crimson patch. She couldn't see anything except bloody leather, but the red spot was spreading too fast.

She reached for the edge of his leather shirt and pulled up that layer, then the cloth one underneath. Finally, she could see his exposed skin. A bitter taste rose up in her throat at the sight of all that blood, but she forced it down. She had to keep Joel alive. She had to.

Blood oozed from the wound, pooling on his skin now that she'd moved the cloth away. She had to stop the bleeding before the life flowed out of his body.

She still held her knife in one fist, and she used it to slice a long strip of leather from the bottom of his outer shirt. Her fingers trembled as she folded the piece several times, then pressed it to his wound.

A groan slipped from Joel, drawing her focus up to his face. Those features she loved had twisted into deep wreaths of pain.

"Do not leave us." She pressed harder on the leather,

clenching her jaw against the break in her voice. She had to turn her fear into action. What should they do next?

"I've made a bed for him by the fire when he can be moved." Susanna knelt across from her. *Dear Susanna.*

Elan nodded, narrowing her focus back to the wound. "I need leaves from the warrior plant to stop the bleeding. In my pack."

Meksem moved toward the bundles, not Susanna as she'd expected. Elan replayed her words. She'd been speaking in her own language, not the white tongue. She'd have to take more care when she spoke so they others could help. They had no time to waste.

When her friend returned with the pouch of dried, crushed leaves, Elan looked to Susanna and spoke words the white woman could understand. "Crush with water."

Susanna nodded and rose. "I'll make a paste for the wound."

Joel lay with his eyes shut, his breathing thick. Only his chest moved with each inhale, not his belly. If not for the strain around his eyes, he might only be sleeping. Her fingers itched to brush the raven strands of hair from his brow, but she dare not take liberties, especially with Caleb and French standing over them.

Beaver Tail and Meksem had gone to finish settling the horses, but her friend stayed well away from the Blackfoot brave. A spear of worry slipped through Elan. Would they punish Meksem? The shot had been an accident, she had no doubt.

But if Joel died from the wound...

No. He couldn't die. She wouldn't let him.

By the time Susanna returned with a poultice to pack the hole in Joel's middle, the bleeding had begun to slow. "We need to see if the bullet went all the way through."

She was right. Elan hadn't treated a gunshot wound herself, but she'd seen other women in camp tend their men after battles against the Blackfoot. One such wound had festered as the brave grew weaker and weaker. Finally one of the shaman opened the gash with a blade and pulled out a small black ball. Only then had the man recovered.

"I'll help turn him over." Caleb moved around to the side where Susanna knelt and crouched in position to pull Joel's shoulder.

Elan sent a glance to his face, but he'd not opened his eyes. How much agony he must be in. *God of the white man, if you're real, please help him.*

As Caleb rolled Joel's shoulder and hip, Joel's face twisted, and he let out a fierce cry that tore through her, wrenching her own heart with his pain.

Susanna worked quickly to pull aside the layers of clothing covering his back. "No bullet hole. Nothing."

Caleb eased Joel back down as Elan processed what the words meant. The ball was still in him. They'd have to pull it out. By cutting the hole open wider? From what she remembered, the other brave had been so feverish and delirious, he'd not known much that happened.

But Joel would feel every part.

"Let's get him to the fire before we worry about removing the bullet." Susanna glanced at the others.

Elan forced herself to focus on that task. Tiny bumps had risen on his bare skin, and his body had begun to shake. They had to keep him warm.

With Caleb at his head and Beaver Tail at his feet, they lifted Joel. His body dipped in the middle, and the clench of his teeth couldn't be mistaken as they carried him.

If only she could do more than move beside him. If only she could take away his pain, or at least stop the movement that surely deepened his agony. She rested her hand on Joel's wrist as they walked. He moved his hand to enclose hers in his. No doubt a desperate cry for any small bit of comfort he could find.

She gave a gentle squeeze, and his grip tightened. Almost painfully tight, but she held on without loosening her own hold.

As they laid him on the furs Susanna had stretched out, his grip loosened, then slipped away in the jostling. The loss pressed on her chest, but she needed both hands now anyway.

She pulled an extra fur up over his legs, and Susanna tucked another over his shoulders and around his arms, covering every part of him except the wound. Red oozed around the edges of the poultice Susanna had laid on the hole. Elan cut another strip of leather, folded it in several layers, then pressed it hard over the wound and the herb, leaning over Joel to keep her force steady.

As she held that position, her eyes kept wandering to his face, which had paled to only a few shades darker than the snow. He'd lost so much of his life-blood. Could his body survive with what he still possessed?

Fight this, Joel. You must fight to live. Tears surged to her eyes. A sting she couldn't allow.

She lifted her gaze to the landscape around them, to the distant river that could be seen even from this position, although a bluff hid much of the view. If only they were there already. If only they'd reached the village where they'd have shelter and a warm fire, nourishing food for themselves and their horses. And a variety of plants to help Joel's body to replenish everything he'd lost.

A wet drop landed on her hand where she pressed down on Joel's wound. Had a tear escaped after all? She looked down, then sniffed, trying to feel through the numbing cold on her face.

She'd not cried.

Another drop splattered on her nose. *No.*

Not rain. Not this too.

CHAPTER 11

*E*lan raised her face to the heavens and stared up at the thick clouds, low and tight, even darker than a usual evening sky. Definitely rain clouds.

"We need to put up a covering." Susanna rose and turned to the others. "Beaver, do we still have the oil cloth?"

As she directed the men, spreading ropes from the trees and pounding poles in the ground, more drops came in an irregular rhythm. Elan grabbed a blanket and held it over Joel like a tent, using the length of her arms to shield as much of his body from the water as possible.

The last thing he needed was for his clothing to grow drenched and freeze. He'd already become wet and cold from lying in the snow, and now the rain would weaken the fire. Thankfully, Caleb and Meksem were working to stretch the makeshift shelter over the fire, too.

If only they had a real lodge for protection.

At last, they'd rigged as much cover as they could manage. Rain fell in steady rhythm around them as she and Susanna huddled next to Joel's pallet. French and Caleb were only partly protected from the freezing wet where they stood halfway under the cover's edges. Meksem and Beaver stood under the trees, but both were surely soaked through by now.

Elan studied her longtime friend, but Meksem wore her warrior face that gave no emotion away. Elan had always hated that expression, and even more so now. Mostly because it meant Meksem was trying too hard to be something she wasn't. She always thought she had to be tougher and smarter than the men.

But why? That was a secret she'd never been able to pull from her friend. Maybe Meksem didn't fully understand the reasons herself.

Now, she was probably retreating into her shell from the pain of having injured a friend. Maybe even killed him. *God of the white man, don't let him die. Please.*

"Are you awake, Joel?" Susanna's question pulled Elan back to their patient.

The tight lines of pain shifted as his mouth opened. "Yes." His eyes remained closed, and he spoke through gritted teeth, the word barely sounding above the din of rain.

Susanna sent Elan a pointed look, then rose and motioned for Elan to come too. They stepped to where the French and Caleb stood, and Susanna motioned for Beaver and Meksem to come near enough to hear. This was to be a parley then.

As soon as all had drawn near, Susanna sent a quick glance toward Joel, then looked at each of the others, moving her gaze from one anxious face to the next. "We need to get that bullet out of him. He also has to stay dry and warm, and he needs water and broth to eat until we determine what's been hit inside him." Her throat worked as she swallowed. "I can use my pa's gunsmithing tools to get the bullet out, but the rest of it will be hard to manage the way he needs it. His body is so weak, if he doesn't have every one of those things, he may not..." Her throat worked. "His body can't..."

Elan had to fight with everything in her to hold back the burn stinging her eyes. Susanna was right, of course. Every part.

They'd have to change him out of anything wet and build up the fire. How long would they need to stay here? Firewood might be hard to manage for several days.

"I think we should try to get him to the Kannah camp." Susanna's words rolled through Elan's mind, and she had to struggle to form them into a clear thought. Move him? How? He wouldn't be able to sit a horse by himself. They'd have to tie him on, and surely that would bring so much pain. And also start the bleeding again.

Elan had seen life fade from men who'd lost less blood than what had already leaked out of Joel.

"We can make a sling for him like we did with Pa." Susanna must have noticed the churning in Elan, for she focused her attention on her. "My father was with us for part of this journey in his last days. He wanted to see the mountains, but he wasn't able to sit up on a horse. Beaver Tail made a sling with poles and furs to hang between two horses. I think it could work for Joel."

But the way Susanna's brows lowered and her lips rolled between her teeth spoke of more uncertainty than what sounded in her tone.

Elan looked around the group. "What think you all?"

Beaver was the first to offer a single tilt of his chin. "Joel can handle it if anyone can."

"He's right." Caleb nodded.

French looked to Meksem. "A half day's ride you think?"

She dipped her chin in confirmation.

Then French looked to Beaver. "Think this rain will stop in the next few hours? The horses will have rested a little."

He peered up at the sky through the moisture running down his cheeks. "Sometime in the night."

Susanna nodded as though the matter were settled firmly in her mind. "We'll ride out at first light." She looked to Elan. "I'd rather wait until we have better light and shelter to take the bullet out. Do you agree?"

A thread of relief slipped through Elan and she nodded. "Before dark tomorrow."

~

*I*f only Elan had something to give Joel to ease the journey. Anything that would take away his pain.

He'd laid in the sling all morning, his eyes pressed tight, jaw clamped, lines marring his brow. The choppy sounds of his breathing rose above the creak of saddle leather and the thump of horse hooves.

He hung between Susanna and Beaver Tail's horses, and now that they were riding on the plain, she rode beside Susanna. This way, she could look over her saddle pack to watch Joel. But every glimpse pressed harder on her chest, tightening the knot coiled in her middle.

Could he manage much more? The last two times they stopped, the wound had begun bleeding anew. She'd pressed hard with fresh leather until the flow stopped, then repacked the hole with yarrow leaves. But maybe it was time she do it again.

She raised a hand. "We should stop again."

Susanna and her brave halted in tandem, but Meksem sent Elan a glare as she turned her mare to face him.

Elan ignored her and slid to the ground. "I need check bleeding." The dog had been walking since their last stop, as the snow wasn't as deep on the plain. He met her the moment she dismounted, staying close by her side as she moved to Joel.

His eyes opened in slits as she slipped between the horses to stand behind him. If there was anything she could do to relieve his pain, she'd do it, but a gentle touch was all she could offer.

She pressed her fingers to his brow. Warm, but not burning. They'd wrapped him in furs to ward off the chill, so that was likely the cause of the warmth she felt. Hopefully.

She ran her hand down his face—letting herself relish the chance to touch as her fingers arrived at his neck. The beat of his blood was fast, what little she could feel. At least he had blood left to flow, but they had to reach camp where she could make a marrow broth for him. Something to regain his strength.

Beside her, Susanna's horse stomped a hoof. She'd best move with more haste. Reaching forward, she shifted the fur covering so she could see his wound. Red soaked the leather strap they'd wrapped around him to hold the poultice in place and slow the bleeding. Swipes of crimson covered his entire belly like the hands of a child playing at painting. But nothing seemed to be oozing from under the bandage.

Joel lifted a hand, and she glanced first at the hand, then at his face to see what he meant by the act. He was watching her through the cracks between his eyelids, but he didn't seem to be trying to say anything.

Maybe he simply needed comfort.

She placed her hand in his, wrapping her fingers around his work-worn palm. He closed her hand in his, enfolding her in his warmth. Even with his strength so low, feeling his touch made her achingly aware of the fact he was very much a man.

A man she wanted to know better.

God of the white man, please give me the chance to know him better. Don't take him away now.

Joel's eyes drifted shut, his hand still wrapped around hers. This time, she let herself follow the urge to brush the hair from his brow. As she stroked her fingertips across his skin, his lips parted. Some of the lines on his face softened.

Only then did awareness sink through her. The rest of the group sat on their horses.

Watching her.

She gave Joel's hand a final squeeze, then slipped her fingers from his, lowering his palm to rest by his side. After covering him again with the fur, she inhaled a steadying breath, then raised her chin toward the trail ahead. "No new bleeding. We ride again."

She didn't dare look into any of the others' faces as she mounted her horse and nodded her readiness to proceed.

They rode onward, toward the glimmering line of water. The Koos-koos-ke river. The one the white men called Clearwater. A little farther downstream should be the Kannah camp they sought.

Would Adam be there? The thought sent a jolt of awareness through her. The urgency to get Joel to a place where they could tend him had consumed every thought for his brother.

What would Adam say about Joel's injury? Would anger burn hot within him toward Meksem for shooting his brother, even though by accident? The others hadn't accused her, but they weren't blood relation.

Suddenly, the appeal of reaching the camp no longer flamed as brightly. But Joel needed help. Once he was healing—for he *would* heal—they could face whatever retaliation Adam might intend toward Meksem.

Even before they reached the river's edge, a group of braves appeared in the distance, riding alongside the water toward them. The strangers pushed their horses into a run, closing the distance quickly.

Beside her horse, the dog raised its ears toward the oncoming riders, but he didn't sprint forward or bark. Someone had taught him manners.

As the braves neared, she could tell none of them wore paint for war, only the black marks to shield their eyes from sun on snow. Elan nudged her horse up to ride beside Meksem in the lead. She would usually have allowed the men to handle the conversation, but she'd met some from this village in the past. Maybe she would know these men.

As Meksem spoke a greeting, she scanned their faces—seven men in all. One in the back struck a chord of recognition in her.

Hemene, her husband's uncle. The man had already seen her and was watching her with sadness in his eyes. That same emotion pressed in her chest. Chuslum had always liked this uncle. She'd not heard he'd come to the Kannah village.

Meksem was explaining about Joel and his need for a place to recover as well as much good medicine. Hemene spoke a quick word she didn't catch, and the man who seemed to be leader of the group nodded.

He turned his horse and motioned for them to follow. Elan breathed out her relief. Help at last.

∾

*A*s soothing as the gentle strokes across his brow felt to Joel, nothing could cover the fire in his belly. He wanted to grip the burning area and curl around it, anything to escape the agony. But every shift—every slight movement—enflamed the burn even more, like throwing kerosene on a fire.

"Can you drink broth now?"

Elan. Her sweet voice flowed through him like a gentle rain, doing its best to quench the heat in his body. Even the lilt of her accent and the rolling cadence she gave each word soothed him. Having her near helped as much as anything could.

He reached for her, not yet putting forth the effort to open his eyes. Her cool hand slid into his, her touch easing his spirit.

"Now open your mouth." Her voice held a smile, as though the contact pleased her, too.

He parted his lips and did his best to open his eyes. The lids weighed so heavily, he could only manage a crack. Enough to see the blurry outline of her form.

The press of wood on his lips came just before a warm liquid dribbled into his mouth. He let it slide around his tongue,

89

pooling behind his teeth and wetting his throat before he forced the effort to swallow. His throat burned with the pain of the first sip, but the next bite she spooned went down easier.

A third time she touched his lips with the spoon, then poured the broth in. He swallowed, and his belly clenched tightly the moment the liquid slid down.

He cried out as a violent pain shot through him, like a massive fist twisting his insides in its fierce grip.

"Joel!"

He barely heard Elan's panicked cry. Nothing could rise over the fiery tongs lighting his stomach.

Somehow, he'd curled into a ball, the pain of moving only a slight distraction from the deeper agony as his stomach tried to spew out the broth. He lay curled on his side, struggling for each breath but managing only slight bits of air.

God, take me. He wasn't sure he could endure much more of this agony.

But Adam. He had to stay alive long enough to find his brother. Adam needed help.

If Joel surrendered to the darkness pressing in even now, would the others continue the search for his brother?

And Elan...the thought of losing her. Of never again seeing her sweet face and those soul-wrenching eyes... Could he relinquish her? Leave her in the same way her first husband had done?

God, if You're there, be with Elan. Help her through her pain. And maybe...don't take me yet.

I'm not ready.

Somehow he had to find a way through this pain. He had to survive. For Adam. For Elan.

CHAPTER 12

*E*lan studied the steady rise and fall of Joel's chest. Deeper breaths than before. Did he finally sleep?

She inhaled her own deep breath, letting her insides quiver as the air struggled to fill her, then eased out in a long exhale.

This first bit of food hadn't gone as well as she'd hoped. He'd managed to swallow sips of water without upset, but his stomach must have been damaged by the bullet. If simple marrow broth caused this much agony, how would he manage anything more?

Maybe once they fished the bullet from the wound, his insides would heal.

The buffalo hide covering the lodge opening shifted, and Susanna stepped inside carrying a leather bucket of water. "The others have the horses settled. Meksem is helping them talk with your uncle and some of the elders. I thought it best they stay occupied while we take care of things in here."

Elan nodded and turned her focus to the other man who lay on a pallet of furs in the lodge. Adam.

He looked so much like his brother, with the same dark hair

and fine-set features. If he opened his eyes, they would probably be just as dark and intense.

But he hadn't opened them. He hadn't awakened at all from his feverish state. Since they'd been shown to this lodge and the men had settled Joel on the pallet beside his brother, she'd built a fire, warmed a marrow broth one of the women gave her, trickled three small bites into Joel's mouth, and sat helplessly beside him as he writhed in pain, finally slipping into the present sleep.

In all that time, Adam hadn't moved more than the slow rise of his chest and the occasional parting of his lips, as though speaking to someone in a dream. The beading of sweat on his brow gave evidence of the heat wracking his body even before she'd pressed fingers to his skin.

Susanna placed the bucket between the men and handed a cloth to Elan. "These are the last of the clean ones. Once we have time, I'll start washing."

Elan dipped the rag in the water, squeezed a little out, then wiped it over Adam's face, cleaning and soothing at the same time. Looking at him felt almost other-worldly, as though looking at Joel, yet...not Joel.

She couldn't stop her wayward gaze from straying back to that very man. Did he even realize his brother lay here beside him? She'd not told him, for she wasn't sure knowing the dangers of Adam's true condition would be good for him. Might the strain push him so far he damaged himself even more?

Susanna knelt on Joel's other side, a small leather pouch in her hands. After unfastening the tie, she unrolled the leather, displaying small pockets with tools protruding from each. "My father was a gunsmith, building and repairing muskets and rifles. This kit holds many of his tools. I think I can get the bullet out with this."

She extracted a tiny pair of metal tongs as long as her finger. "I'll need a minute to clean everything I think we might use."

Elan dipped her cloth in the cool water again, then draped the rag over Adam's brow before turning back to Joel. Already, images of what Susanna would have to do had restarted the churning in her middle.

Elan had to stay strong. Had to do everything she could to help Joel pull through this. If she could have done the same to save her sweet daughter and husband, she would have.

Anything. And that was exactly what she would do now for Joel.

Working together, they rolled Joel on his back, then Elan cleaned the skin around his wound. Already, the flesh surrounding the hole had begun to turn red, the ragged edges swelling. Joel seemed to sleep through it all. The pain must have pushed him into a black haze.

"After we get the bullet out, I have a garlic mixture that will help keep it from festering." Susanna bent low as she peered into the hole.

"My uncle's wife has more yarrow. Also help."

"Good." Susanna inserted two thin silver rods into the wound. "Can you hold these apart to let as much light into the hole as you can?"

Swallowing down the bitter taste in her mouth, Elan took the tiny pieces in her fingertips and stretched the wound as wide as she could manage. Joel groaned.

God of the white man, take the pain from him. Give us good favor to remove the bullet.

Elan barely breathed as Susanna worked, burying the tiny tool in the dark recesses of the bloody wound as she leaned first one way, then another.

Her steady murmurs gave a running flow of her progress. "I found it." Her brow wrinkled and her lips parted. "I can't... It won't..." Then her mouth pinched, and she leaned a different angle.

Elan did her best to hold her hands steady and away from the path of the light shining into the bullet hole.

At last, Susanna inhaled an audible breath as her body froze. The intense concentration on her face pulled the tension even tighter in Elan's body. Little by little, Susanna eased her hands upward.

Elan spread the wound even wider, doing everything she could to keep the ball from brushing the edges, from knocking out of the tool's grip as Susanna raised it from the hole.

When she'd just cleared the opening, the pliers jerked, and the ball shot sideways.

Elan jumped back, the tension that had coiled in her shoulders springing loose like a wild cat attacking. She bit down hard to keep a yelp from slipping out.

"No." Susanna lunged toward the wound, covering the hole with both hands. The ball rolled off Joel and landed harmlessly on the pressed dirt floor.

Silence settled for a long moment, and Elan pressed a hand to her chest to slow her racing heart.

Susanna let out a laugh as she straightened. "I could just see it rolling back into the wound, where I'd have to fish it out all over again."

Her grin was so bright, her relief so obvious, a smile bubbled out onto Elan's own face. "You did it."

Susanna laughed again, a bright, musical laugh. "I can't believe it, but we did."

For another moment, Elan let herself savor the chance to settle her nerves. So much fear had built inside her.

Now that the bullet was removed, he really had the chance to heal. If he rested and she saw to his every need, maybe he would pull through this.

She might not lose him yet.

∾

*E*very part of Joel ached, but at least he was alive. The fire in his belly had finally dulled to a low burn. Now, a parching thirst consumed his mouth.

He pried his eyes open, and this time he could see more details than before. Nothing moved around him, but the light was dim, maybe the faint glow of early morning. Or...maybe that glow was a fire.

He turned his head to see better. Yes, a campfire and...he squinted at what lay beyond. Was he in a lodge? This felt so much like the smoky interior of the lodge he'd shared with Caleb, French, and Beaver Tail last winter in Beaver's village.

Did that mean...? He lifted his head to get a better look, but fire shot through his gut again, fiercer than any blow he'd ever experienced from a fist.

He dropped his head back and focused on inhaling steady breaths, not moving anything except his lungs. At last, his mind cleared enough to think. Had they reached the village where Adam had gone?

Was his brother here, even now? Where were the others?

He focused hard on his surroundings, staring up at the hide stretched over him, the hole in the center he could barely see at the corner of his vision.

Sounds slipped into his awareness. The murmur of distant voices, probably people outside the lodge. The crackle of the fire, a small one from the faint noises. Steady breathing. Not snoring, but the slight rhythm of someone small. Elan?

Keeping his body still, he eased his chin to one side, toward the fire. His vision blurred again, but he gave himself time to focus, sweeping his gaze slowly around the area.

A lump of something sat nearby, maybe an arm's reach away from him. As he focused on the object, an outline took shape. A person. He tried to make out Elan's shape, lying on her back, face pointed upward. He could see the rise and fall of the chest, but that certainly wasn't the form of a woman.

He studied the profile of the face. That flat, sloped brow, the deep-set eyes, the nose slightly bigger than Joel's own, but exactly the same rounded shape. Under the thick growth of beard would be a slight cleft in his chin. And if he opened his eyes, the rich orange-green color would make anyone looking at him stop and stare.

Adam.

As certainty sank through him, determination flooded his veins. He had to touch his brother. Had to know for sure that really was air lifting his chest.

He swallowed to summon moisture into his parched throat. He didn't manage much, but hopefully enough. "Adam." He croaked the single word, his voice not sounding at all like usual. But Adam would know him, surely.

The figure didn't move, only the slight lifting of his chest with each breath.

Fear clutched in Joel's chest. "Adam." This time he sounded more like himself. But still, no movement from his brother.

Summoning his strength, Joel reached across the short distance between them. His fingers barely touched the fur the man lay on. Joel stretched farther, gritting his teeth against the pain. He had to inch sideways before his hand closed over an arm.

Warmth emanated through the buckskin tunic. A good sign.

Joel gave it a shake. "Adam, wake up."

The man moaned, a sound Joel had never been so grateful to hear in his life. Even more than the time when they were boys and Adam was thrown from the Andalusian stallion he wasn't supposed to have been riding. The horse had stomped Adam's body so many times, the doctor didn't think he'd make it. The priest came and read the last rights, but Adam clung to life. For weeks he'd lain in bed, Joel by his side most days, telling him stories and keeping his imagination occupied so his body could heal.

Together, they'd pulled through. Now they would again.

Joel worked himself closer to his brother, rolling onto his side so he could see Adam better and use both hands. He gripped Adam's arm again and gave it a good shake. More than warm…enough heat rose through the leather to cook a slab of meat.

"You have to wake up, Adam. It's me, Joel. I finally found you."

His brother's lips parted, cracking open with a painful groan. He likely needed something to drink too. And some bear fat to help the chapping.

Joel strained to hear what he might say. His jaw worked, but no sound emerged.

The lodge flap shifted, letting in the soft light of morning. An outline filled the opening, then a soft gasp sounded. "Joel."

Elan. *Thank you, God.* He exhaled the prayer as she stepped in quickly and moved to his side. The dog padded beside her.

"He needs water. We both do." The strength he'd managed before sluiced out of him now, and he could barely hold up his head.

"Lay first. Then water." She gripped his shoulder and pushed with enough effort to guide him back to his fur pallet. But he couldn't allow that.

"No. Let me lay beside him. I can help him." He *had* to help Adam. Had to bring him back to life. His brother was the only family he had left.

Elan moved to Joel's feet, and the bottom part of his pallet shifted sideways toward Adam. He tried to help her by lifting his legs, but the effort felt like a dagger plunging into his belly.

"I do." She rested a hand on his leg to still him, then straightened and stepped to where his head had laid on the fur.

After shifting the head, then moving back to the foot again, then to the head again, she finally had his fur in place next to his brother's. She gripped his arm to help him roll flat on his back, and her hand sent a warmth through him, easing his angst the way her touch always did.

At last he lay flat, every bit of his energy spent and his belly burning.

"Water now." She moved to Adam's other side and bent down over a bucket.

"Adam first." He turned his head so he could watch her as she knelt by his brother's side with a wooden bowl and spoon. "What's wrong with him? Has he woken at all?"

She lifted the spoon to Adam's mouth. "Not wake. Skin burning."

He reached out to touch his brother's hand again. Like touching a hot coal.

Fear twisted in his belly, churning with the pain until he had to fight to keep from spewing out what little his stomach contained.

Elan's touch was gentle as she coaxed water down Adam's throat. She dabbed his lips dry, then rubbed grease over them before Joel even remembered to ask her. She had a special way about her, a nurturing spirit that softened every touch, soothing with each ministration. He'd noticed it before, but not so distinctly as now, watching her work over his brother's quiet body.

God, help him. Not for me, but for Adam. Make him well.

Elan moved to his side next, the dog following her every step, and Joel didn't have the strength to stop his gaze from doing the same. The flickering firelight cast her tawny face in a rich copper, illuminating the strong planes.

She raised the spoon of water to his mouth. He parted his dry lips, and the cool liquid filled his dry mouth like steady rain after a long drought. In truth, the water felt so rich as it spread over his tongue and down his throat, his senses burned with the goodness of it.

He kept his gaze on her face, honing in on her eyes. Wide, but coming together at the outer edges in a delicate crease, just enough to give her a bit of intrigue.

She refilled her spoon and raised it to his lips again, her attention focused on her work. As she poured the water in, her gaze lifted to his eyes—and froze there, like a deer sensing the hunter's presence.

He should drop his gaze and set her at ease. But his weary body wouldn't follow through with the thought. Instead, he held her look, letting her see him as he was—the raw essence he'd been stripped down to. A man desperate to save his brother, the last bit of family he had left. Yet not the last, not really. Hadn't Beaver Tail and Caleb and French all proved as faithful as family? Susanna, too, although she was new to their group.

And now Elan. Part of him wanted to open himself to know her better. Wanted to see what could happen if he allowed her into his heart.

But would she want that? Given the pain she'd been through less than a year before with the loss of her husband and child?

All this she probably saw in his eyes, as perceptive as she was. What did she think? Her gaze gave nothing back. At least, nothing he had the strength to decipher.

He let his heavy eyelids drift closed. Later, he would try to make sense of it. When he wasn't so weak. When Adam recovered.

CHAPTER 13

*E*lan glanced up as Meksem stepped into the lodge, accompanied by a gust of fresh, icy air and blessed daylight. She couldn't help but peek through the door flap before it settled into place. Being in the open air for so long must have spoiled her. She'd never before chafed after only a half day in a lodge tending someone in her care.

Her gaze drifted to Joel, his face softened in slumber. He'd slept a great deal today, a restful sleep, not plagued by excessive pain. A good sign. If she could only get more than two spoonfuls of broth down him before his belly refused any more. Living on water alone, his strength would fade quickly.

Like Adam's had. She slid her focus to the older brother. She'd finally stopped feeling as though she were in a dream when she looked at him, his features so similar to Joel's—yet not. His sunken cheeks and pale skin were only a few of the differences. At least he kept down the water and broth she spooned into his mouth. If only the heat would leave his skin.

If only he'd open his eyes. At times, he seemed aware of what was happening around him. He responded to voices—especially Joel's voice—with a parting of his lips or a faint groan.

But he never truly awoke. *God of the white man, show me how to help him.*

Meksem stepped to the feet of both men, her gaze surveying first Joel, then Adam. She wore that expression impossible to read. The one she used when trying not to let others see how hard she was working to be what she considered good enough.

Elan pushed up to standing. It was time to give Meksem a chance to work through what had happened out there in the mountains. The accidental shooting. She'd kept herself distant from them all since then, as though afraid getting too near would cause more harm. Or maybe she was just afraid to face what she'd done.

Elan moved to her friend's side. The dog jumped to its feet and padded along beside her. "Will you stay with them while I step outside?"

Her friend stiffened, the action slight enough Elan wouldn't have seen it if she hadn't been watching. Meksem sent Elan a look, finally lowering that stiff expression she wore as a mask. Wariness joined with something that could be fear in her gaze.

Elan placed a gentle hand on her arm and spoke quietly enough that neither man would overhear, even if they could make out their language. "He doesn't blame you. It was an accident."

Meksem shifted her gaze back to Joel, and her shoulders gave a quick rise and fall, as though she were struggling to maintain control of herself. She nodded, an act so fierce, Elan's heart ached for her friend. Would she ever learn she didn't have to always be the strong one? Always working to make sure others only saw her toughness, the fierce mask of a warrior.

Elan sent a gentle stroke down her friend's arm, then glanced back at the men. "Try to spoon water down any time Joel wakes. Maybe you can talk to Adam while you're here. We need to wake him up."

Without waiting to give Meksem a chance to run, Elan turned and strode to the door flap.

Her eyes struggled to adjust to the bright sunlight, and she paused to take in the normal sounds of a thriving village drifting around her. Children calling to each other in play at the far end of town. Their high-pitched voices rang around the lodges, shooting a fresh arrow through her heart.

Alikkees had loved to play with her group of friends. Dolls, catch-the-pine cone, anything at all. She'd loved people, and people had loved her. With that dazzling smile and irresistible laugh, she charmed everyone she met.

But no one had loved her nearly as much as Elan had. Alikkees had been her entire world. She'd done everything she could so her daughter would know how much she was loved. At least, Elan didn't have that regret.

Two women approached, each carrying a basket draped over an arm. The older was her uncle's wife, Kaya'aton'my, a woman with stooped shoulders and a quick gate who'd proved already she could accomplish more in a morning than women half her age. The other didn't look familiar, younger for certain, seeming barely old enough to be the mother of the young child on her hip.

As the women approached, Elan sent them a smile. The expression felt almost foreign on her face, maybe because of the worry for Joel and Adam that had shrouded her these past two days. Maybe simply because her eyes still strained from the sunlight reflecting off snow.

The lad peered from his mother's shoulder as the women stopped in front of her. He couldn't have lived more than two summers, and his hair barely reached his shoulders in uneven layers. His face still bore the rounded look of the youngest ones, and his wide eyes danced with life. He might be quiet in his mother's arms now, but she'd seen that active look before. After another summer, he'd be fleet of foot and doing his best to keep up with the oldest in the group.

"The white men still sleep?" Kaya'aton'my watched her for an answer.

Elan nodded. "Adam still doesn't wake. Joel has been awake but sleeps now. He still can't drink more than two sips of broth."

Kaya'aton'my thrust the basket into her hands. "Make drink good for his belly."

Elan glanced inside at the bundles of dried leaves. "I steep them in water?"

The older woman nodded. "Can cook in camas bread when he is ready to eat. Until then, boil in water for him to drink."

Her aunt turned. "Your others with horses." She pointed to the north side of the camp, where they'd seen clusters of spotted horses when they first rode in.

Kaya'aton'my marched away, intent on her next task. The younger woman didn't leave with her but gave Elan a shy smile as she held out her own basket. "I have been baking camas root for many sleeps to make them sweet and thought your people might want some. Since you came overmountain, you may not have much food left."

The rich, savory scent of the delicacy wafted from the leather bundle in the basket. The others would appreciate these, no doubt. Chuslum always had. In fact, the first time he'd complimented Elan was when she'd toiled over her oven for many sleeps to bake the root sweet for him.

A niggle tugged inside her, and she glanced back at the young woman. "I thank you, and I'm sure the others will too. I am called Elan."

"I am Otskai."

Elan couldn't help looking at the little one. "And who is this?" She rubbed a hand over the boy's back.

The lad turned to her, wide eyes studying her.

"We call him Pikun-hazual, River Boy. When he was barely

able to walk, he got away from me, and I found him in the river, swimming like one of the salmon."

While still watching Elan with that wide, intense stare, he thrust his arms toward her.

Elan almost stepped back. Surely he didn't want her—a stranger—to hold him.

But Otskai leaned toward her, silent consent to her son's request.

So be it. But as she slipped her hands around the little waist and pulled him to her, a weight settled on her chest so hard it pushed away any chance of drawing breath. Pain sliced through her heart, all the way to her very core. She'd not held a child since Alikkees, and she'd been right to keep herself away. This wonderful, terrible agony was too much.

River Boy wrapped his pudgy legs around her and settled his hands on her shoulders, staring at her with such a sober expression in his dark eyes.

"Hello." She offered him a smile, an act that came easily despite the wrenching inside her. "Did you help your mother bake the camas? I'll bet they taste good, don't they?"

He offered a single nod, then wrapped his arms around her neck in what felt dangerously close to a hug. Heat seared her eyes, and she tucked her face into the crook of his neck. Maybe to cover the threat of tears, but as she inhaled his little boy scent and brushed her cheek against the softness of his hair, the real reason became achingly clear.

This was home.

Even though this lad wasn't her Alikkees, the touch and scent of him, the unrestrained trust little ones were so apt to grant, all came together in a feeling of wholeness she hadn't savored since that last awful day.

River Boy squirmed, and she straightened, pulling away from the lad. He settled himself on her hip and pointed in the distance. "Horses."

Elan blinked back the last of the moisture from her eyes and turned to Otskai. "My friends are with the horses, and that's where I was going." She motioned down to the dog at her side. He looked up at her, tongue lolling in a slow pant. "We both need a walk. Would you like to come? We can all share the camas together."

A flush slipped into the young woman's face as a tiny smile appled her cheeks. "We will come."

Something about the smile brought back a reminder of what she'd planned to ask the woman. As they walked along, Elan made her tone casual. "You and your husband are both of the Kannah band?"

She nodded. "I was promised to Motsqueh when young, and he was a great warrior among these people. Now he has been gone two summers."

Elan glanced over at her as the familiar weight of sadness pressed down. "I am sorry for your loss."

Otskai nodded but kept her gaze pointed ahead. She didn't seem burdened by pain. Were two years enough to ease the fierce blade of loss? But then, this woman had only lost a husband, not a child. Not the whole of her heart.

But that wasn't fair. Perhaps Otskai had loved her husband. She certainly spoke of him with respect. And she'd been forced to raise her son without a father.

She glanced back. "Have you taken a new husband?"

Otskai shook her head. "I don't plan to if I can make our way on my own."

They'd reached the edge of the village, and a flat plain stretched before them. Grass poked up from the ankle-deep snow, and their horses hobbled in the midst of the open land and tore into the stalks like ravenous wolves. Caleb and French worked among the animals, Caleb brushing one of the pack mares and French bent to work over one of the geldings' hooves.

"Horses." River Boy reached toward the animals.

He didn't squirm to get down, so Elan kept him in her arms as they trekked across the field. The silence drifted easily between them, and Elan focused on deep, cleansing breaths of the chilly air.

"The injured one, he will live?" Otskai's voice came out hesitant, as though she hated to break the peacefulness with a reminder of troubles.

Elan's middle pinched. "He will." *I hope.* She didn't say that last part, but she couldn't stop herself from thinking it. Surely since Joel hadn't grown worse, he would recover. They'd gotten the bullet out, after all.

And she'd prayed to the white man's God. The God who Susanna and Beaver Tail and Caleb all spoke to as if He were standing beside them. If Joel recovered, would it mean their God was real? In truth, if she didn't already believe He existed, would she have even prayed? Yet, having an all-powerful being Who cared enough about His people to hear and grant their petitions seemed too wonderful to be real.

"What of the other man, the one who came in with those Tii-wel-ka." She used the old word for the Shoshone, the one that named them as enemies. And her tone held a distaste Elan had heard all her life.

Yet now, the bias rankled. Just because The People and the Shoshone had warred off and on for many years didn't mean that every Shoshone was evil. Those they'd met on the trail had been a bad sort, but surely there was some good among the tribe. As Joel said, *I've always tried to judge a man according to his own actions, not what people or tribe he was born into.*

Otskai was watching her, clearly waiting for an answer. Elan scrambled to remember what she'd said. "Adam? His skin is hot and he doesn't wake. I give him water and broth, but I don't know how else to help him."

A fresh wave of fear clutched in her chest. Speaking aloud

his condition and what little she was doing to help brought her lack to glaring light. She turned to Otskai as desperation churned inside her. "My uncle says there is no healer in this village, but is there no one else who can help? Anyone who can direct me?"

If Joel lost his brother after fighting so hard to find him, what would that do to his own chance of survival? The thought of losing Joel swirled in her throat until she couldn't swallow. Could barely breathe.

Otskai was watching her, gaze narrowed as though she were trying to decipher a challenge. "One of them is yours?"

The words didn't make sense, and she replayed them in her mind. One of the men? Her...husband? Maybe the woman only meant a family member.

Either way, Elan shook her head, fighting the heat flaming up her neck. "No. Meksem and I met Joel and the others in the mountains. They needed a guide to find Joel's brother, so we agreed to help. I did not know any of them. I'm not..." She inhaled a steadying breath. "My warrior died with our daughter at the beginning of summer."

The moment the words came out, she wanted to snatch them back. Why had she shared such a personal detail with this woman she'd just met?

Otskai turned forward again, toward the horses they would soon reach. "That is why you carry sadness like a cloak." Then she slid a glance to the boy who rode on Elan's hip, his chubby cheeks rounded in a smile. "And also why my son has taken to you. You possess the touch of a mother."

She should respond, but that too-familiar burn had crept back into her eyes, so she kept her face forward.

Otskai touched her arm, drawing them both to a halt. Elan forced herself to look at the woman.

Compassion glimmered in her gaze. "It won't always be so hard. Life will continue, and one day you'll want to live again too. You'll learn who you are without them. Don't give up before that."

This time, the tears were impossible to fight back. They swarmed her eyes, blurring her vision. How did Otskai know that was how she felt? She'd lost herself when she'd lost Alik-kees and Chuslum. Missing them was eating her from the inside out, but almost as bad was the sense of being a stranger to herself. Those two had been her world, and now she was adrift in a place she didn't know, forced to carry on without a purpose.

Otskai squeezed her arm, and in that moment, she proved herself no longer a stranger. The connection between them, no matter how new, would be strong and lasting.

A good thing, for she had a feeling she'd be needing a friend soon. The trouble was far from over.

CHAPTER 14

*S*omeone lingered around him.

Joel's body tensed as the sensation prickled even before he opened his eyes. He strained to hear but could make out only Adam's light intakes. Steady enough to prove his brother hadn't awakened yet.

So who else was here? Not, Elan. Somehow, he always knew when she was near. Maybe the way her sweet spirit warmed the air around her. Maybe the way his body quickened to her presence.

He cracked his eyelids enough to see but hopefully not give evidence he was awake. Not until he knew who was here and why.

Probably the visitor was friendly, maybe even Beaver Tail. French and Caleb wouldn't be able to stay so quiet, but Beaver certainly could. He'd honed the skill so well he could probably sneak up on a wildcat undetected.

As his vision adjusted to the dimness, a form took shape on the other side of Adam. The petite figure kneeling beside his brother looked nothing like Beaver Tail.

Meksem. She held herself like a warrior, tall and confident. And so silent.

He opened his eyes fully, and her head lifted. Probably noticing even his small movement.

"He still hasn't awakened." His voice sounded loud in the stillness, and raspy.

She looked back at his brother, and Joel turned his head to better see that familiar profile. Eyes still closed. *God, why won't he wake up? What do I need to do?*

He'd already done everything he could think of. Nothing made his brother come to life. If God was real... If all those stories he'd had stuffed down him as a boy were true, couldn't the Almighty heal Adam? He wasn't even dead like Lazarus had been.

"You asked him to wake?" Meksem spoke with a much heavier accent than Elan, her tongue wrapping around each word individually so he had to replay her statement in his mind to ease the sounds together into a sentence. In truth, that was the most he'd ever heard her say at one time.

Now that her meaning came clear, a wave of frustration washed through him. "Yes, I've asked him. I've told him where he's at and what's happening. I've told him he won't see the spotted horses unless he wakes up. Nothing helps."

Meksem didn't answer. Maybe she didn't understand everything he'd said. She merely kept her gaze on Adam's face. In the dim light, he couldn't read her expression. In *good* light, he usually couldn't read her expression. The woman could keep her face straighter than a swindler.

Then she reached out and brushed her fingers across his brother's brow. Maybe feeling for fever, but there was a tenderness in the touch he'd never seen from this warrior woman.

"Adam." Her voice was soft. Coaxing. "Wake, Adam." With her accent, the words had a quality that seemed almost angelic.

And just like Lazarus back in Biblical days, Adam's eyelids

fluttered, then lifted.

Joel's heart leaped, and he struggled to turn on his side to see better. He didn't dare speak lest the miracle before him disappear.

Adam stared upward, his gaze unfocused. Then he blinked, and his eyes flicked toward Meksem. The two stared at each other.

For a long moment, their gazes held, and a layer of tension seemed to settle in the room. Was she spooked by Adam's eyes? Maybe he should have warned the others. Their orange hue could be unnerving at first.

But Adam seemed just as fixed on her. Whatever was passing between the two of them would have to wait. Joel had come too far and worried too long to hold off any longer.

"Adam."

His brother jerked his head toward him, eyes widening. His mouth parted, then closed, as though trying to summon words. "Joel?" The voice that came out rasped like a two-hundred-year-old man.

Joel reached out and fumbled for his brother's hand. "You're alive. We found you. How do you feel?"

Adam blinked, then his gaze lifted. "Like I'm..." The words rasped so much he paused to clear his throat, then winced with the act. Probably had a splitting headache. "Like I'm coming back from the dead."

Adam had woken up. The wonder of it—the miracle of it—was just now settling over Joel. He couldn't stop the chuckle that broke through, even though the movement sent a fresh shot of fire through his belly. "You're not far from the truth. We weren't sure you were going to pull through."

"We?" Adam turned back to Meksem, who was still watching him with her intense stare.

Joel waited a breath to see if she wanted to introduce herself, but when she didn't speak, he took the initiative. "This is

Meksem. She and her friend, Elan, have been traveling with us as guides. The others—Caleb and French—are outside with the horses."

He had so much to catch his brother up on. "And Beaver Tail. He's a friend from a Blackfoot tribe we spent last winter with. You'll like him. And his new wife Susanna. We met her and her father by the Great Falls, but her father passed away a few months ago."

Now he was rambling, and Adam simply stared at him, eyes narrowed as he worked to take in the mass of information Joel was spraying at him. Not yet the quick-witted brother Adam had always been, full of life and never one to back down from an adventure.

Had the fever and sickness addled his mind permanently? Or was he simply weak and trying to get his bearings?

Joel reached out and rested a palm on his brother's brow. Warm, but not burning like he'd been when they first found him.

He glanced at Meksem. "Can we get him something to eat? Maybe that broth Elan's been feeding him?"

Meksem glanced around, her eyes taking on a hint of apprehension. "I get Elan." Then she rose in a single lithe movement and left the lodge.

Joel almost chuckled at her response. She and Elan couldn't be more different. So much so, the friendship between them seemed unlikely. Elan the gentle nurturer, Meksem the fierce warrior.

He turned his focus back to his brother. "You'll like Elan. She has a healing touch." A touch that had certainly brought Joel back to life. Now that Adam had awakened, too, his world finally felt right. Maybe for the first time in years. "I can't wait to hear about your travels, but first, any idea what made you so sick?"

Adam blinked, shifting his gaze upward again. Then he

squinted and raised a hand to squeeze the bridge of his nose as he pressed his eyes shut. "It's all a blurry haze." He dropped his hand and looked back at Joel and spoke in their native tongue. "Can we speak Spanish? Maybe it will help if my mind doesn't have to translate first."

"*Sí.*" Worry wove through Joel's chest. "Rest now." He continued in the language they'd learned in their earliest years. "You'll have time to remember later."

Adam's eyes drifted shut.

His brother's breathing grew steady again, but Joel's own body was wound too tightly to rest. The regular rise and fall of Adam's chest soothed the tightness in his own as his mind played back through the events from right before his brother had awakened.

Had God answered his prayer? It certainly seemed unusual that Adam would awaken so soon after Joel had lifted up that desperate plea. But what part had Meksem played in resurrecting his brother? Even a thick-headed male like him had noticed the connection of…something…that sparked between them.

Maybe God had used the woman? If so, what did that mean for Adam and this fierce Indian maiden?

Time would tell. As long as they could keep Adam on the mend. If not…

He couldn't even let himself think what he'd do if his brother took another turn for the worse.

~

*J*oel was sitting up.

Elan couldn't remember the last time she'd been this relieved. This grateful. *Thank you, God of the white man.*

She scooped broth from the stew into a bowl and turned to

where Joel sat beside his brother. Both men were propped against rolled furs, joining with the rest of the group around the lodge fire as Caleb recounted the hunt the men had gone on that day.

"I'm sure I hit that elk, but never could find him. No blood trail or anything." His brow furrowed. "Would have been nice to have fresh meat again."

Joel had been watching his friend but turned his gaze to Elan as she approached. His dark eyes shimmered in the firelight, and his mouth tipped up a little on one side. He seemed lighter these past two days since his brother woke up, as though a weight had lifted off his chest. He still carried an intensity, but the fierce determination—almost desperation—that used to drive his every move had lessened.

Now, seeing the light in his eyes directed toward her made something flip in her middle. She couldn't help but smile back. In truth, she'd not felt this happy in many moons.

He took the bowl from her hands, his fingers brushing hers in the process. She straightened, hating to back away. But she had no reason to linger in front of him, especially with the others sitting with them around the fire.

At least he was able to keep the broth down now. The sage leaves her aunt had given them helped more than Elan expected.

A blessing, Susanna called the plant. A nice word, that. An unexpected gift from God sent to help.

She turned to scan the group as the men's conversation continued. French and Caleb had joined in with a group of braves from the village, but only one of the men had brought back game to show for the day's work.

The rest had more than a few stories, which fed the conversation, if not their bellies.

"Sit, Elan. The work is done. You need to eat, too." Joel patted the fur on the ground beside him. Caleb scooted over to make room for her.

She glanced around once more. Everyone had food, including Susanna, who'd already settled in beside Beaver Tail with her own stew and camas bread. Even the dog lay beside Adam, chewing a marrow bone. The animal had rarely left her side since they'd arrived in this camp, but now he seemed content with Adam stroking him.

She turned to scoop her own food. As she settled in beside Joel, her knee rested against his leg. The space was tight, which justified the touch. She could move if she wanted to, but the single connection made her want to scoot closer to him, not farther away.

The others talked for a while, both about the day's events and what lay ahead for the next day. Joel stayed quiet, but his steady presence beside her eased the tangle in her chest so she could relax. It was a wonder how much of their conversation she could understand now. Even Meksem seemed to follow along and offered a few words about what she'd heard one of the hunters say.

"Have you seen the big herds of Palouse horses yet?" Adam still looked pale as he lay propped by furs, but a spark had come into his eyes.

French nodded. "There are a few penned around here, but we saw a big herd in the distance when we first rode out. Did you know these two ride spotted horses?" He motioned to Elan then Meksem, who sat on Adam's other side, tucked between the dog and Susanna.

Adam turned his uncanny orange eyes toward Meksem. "You do? Tell me about them. Do they have the full spots spread all over or only on the rump? What special abilities have you found in them?"

Meksem didn't smile very often, but the corners of her mouth danced up. "White spots on rump. Can ride longer than others."

"She's tellin' the truth there." Caleb leaned forward. "The

horses were all half-starved by the time we made it through the mountains, but the mares these gals ride could go twice as long as ours. And they'd already made the trek through the mountains once just before."

"Running Elk say bring horses to camp when sun two fingers high." Meksem held two fingers sideways as though measuring how far the sun had risen above the horizon.

"Tomorrow?" Adam sat straighter. "They're bringing the spotted horses here tomorrow?" Excitement laced his tone, but then his expression twisted as a cough tore from his throat.

"Why are they bringin' them in during the winter?" Caleb tipped his head. "Do you have much trouble with horse stealin' among the villages?"

Meksem shook her head. "Many horses. No need to steal."

A sigh eased from Adam. "Must be nice."

Maybe Elan should have joined in the conversation, but watching the others, especially with Meksem participating as part of the group, fed contentment over her like a warm fur on a chilly night. Especially with Joel at her side.

She glanced at him, and he met her gaze with warmth in his dark eyes. If only she could spend many more nights just like this. Surrounded by friends and sitting beside the man she'd come to care about far more than was good for her.

What were his plans now that he'd found Adam? She'd heard the brothers talking for long stretches as they recovered side-by-side. Everything seemed to be recounting the time they'd spent apart though. No plans for the future that she'd heard. Would they go back east? The white men always did. They might stay through the winter, but in the spring they always left.

If Joel asked, could she find the courage to go with him? To risk her heart to love again, when she now knew how quickly that love could be crushed in a single blow? He probably wouldn't ask.

But if he did, would she dare take the risk?

CHAPTER 15

"*H*ere, lean on my shoulder."

Joel gritted his teeth as he did his best to straighten, holding tight to Beaver Tail with one hand and clamping his other arm around his middle. His belly twisted as if a giant claw were trying to pull his insides out, but he had to stand up.

Little by little, he pulled himself upright. Mostly. He hunched over like an *anciano*, but at least he could walk. Still, he couldn't bring himself to loosen the hand holding his insides inside.

If Meksem walked into the lodge right now, he'd have trouble being as understanding as he'd been trying to be.

One stray bullet. What were the chances it would land in his gut? Apparently, pretty good.

And this wasn't the first time he'd been shot on this journey. Not one of the other men had so much as a knick from a hunting knife, but he'd been shot *twice*. Both times in the belly, and *both* of them accidents.

Either God had a cruel sense of humor, or He didn't care at all.

But then a memory slipped in...his prayer for Adam right before his brother had awakened. Was that merely chance? Another *accident?*

Sounds drifted in from outside—the whinny of a horse, the voices of men.

Joel released Beaver's shoulder as the man turned to help Adam, who was already rolling onto his knees.

"Careful." Beaver gripped his brother's arm and eased him up to standing.

Adam's face had turned pale, his breathing heavy and quick. Maybe they were pushing his healing too quickly. Perhaps he should stay abed another day.

But with a herd of the renowned Palouse horses meandering just outside the camp, Adam wouldn't be kept from seeing them. Hadn't everything he'd gone through for this day proved his determination? Pig-headed brother that he was.

The lodge flap drew back, and Elan's pretty form filled the space, her ever-present companion padding along at her side. She tied the door covering open, allowing daylight and noise to stream in.

Adam released Beaver's arm and shuffled toward the outdoors. Thankfully, Beaver Tail stayed by his side, especially as Adam's gait weaved a little.

Elan and the dog stepped to the side so the two men could exit. As much as he wanted to see Adam's reaction to the herd— and wanted to see the horses, too, for that matter—Joel paused when he reached her.

A smile tugged her mouth, lighting her face and making her even more beautiful. His chest squeezed. How could he leave her when they moved on? Did he even want to move on? So much had to be settled, but what he knew for now was that he couldn't have walked past her if he'd tried.

"You need help to walk out?" One corner of her mouth tipped up.

Her words tugged a grin from him. "If I did, you'd be the one I'd want to help me."

She ducked her chin as a flush stole over her tawny face. As cute as the look was, he certainly didn't want her embarrassed to be near him.

He motioned toward the dog. "He doesn't leave your side much, does he?"

Her gaze followed his. "A good friend." She reached down to stroke the dog's head. The animal stared at her with a besotted gaze, not that Joel could blame him.

"Have you named him?"

She tipped her head to look up at him, still petting the pup. "Sometimes I call him Little One, but he needs better."

Joel searched his mind for some possible options. "Maybe... Friend? What's your word for that?"

A glimmer touched her eyes, and she straightened, looking at him now with a funny quirk on her lips. As though she was trying to hold in a laugh. Had his suggestion been that awful?

"Elan." Her lips pursed into a cupid's bow as he tried to figure out what she meant. Finally, she spoke again. "Elan means friendly."

Her meaning struck him like a stiff wind, and he couldn't help a chuckle. Then a nod. Yes, she was well-named. She might be reserved, but she'd already proved herself a friend anyone would want by their side.

The searing in his belly kept his chuckle short, stealing his breath. He worked to keep the pain off his face. Finally, he regained enough composure to speak. "That name's taken then. Any other thoughts?"

Her pretty mouth rolled as her gaze wandered in thought. "Maybe another way to say it—companion. Lautua." She glanced down at the dog. "Lautua?"

He perked his ears at her.

Joel nodded. "I think he likes it." As much as he'd like to

stand and talk with Elan all day, they did need to get outside. He touched her elbow. "Show me the horses. I want to see Adam's reaction."

Elan turned, and his hand slipped off her arm as she moved ahead of him through the lodge opening.

The moment Joel stepped outside, an icy wind brushed his face, filling his nostrils with the scent of horseflesh. Their lodge sat near the northeast corner of camp, beside the stretch of plains now filled with meandering horses. Spots spread as far as he could see. Some animals bore black or brown dots scattered over their entire bodies. Others more like Elan and Meksem's horses, dark colored with patches of white hairs sprinkled over their rumps and sometimes the rest of their bodies. In truth, not one animal looked exactly like the next.

Adam and Beaver Tail had paused at the edge of the gathering. The sight of the vast herd—at least a hundred horses—was so much to take in. But Adam was probably cataloging each animal in that quick mind of his.

Then he was moving forward, approaching a horse with brown spots sprinkled across its frame, including one splashed over its right eye. Adam greeted the animal in that special way he had with horses, letting it sniff him, breathing into its nostrils his own greeting—just the way horses did with each other. He'd spent so much time with horses, he understood their language and spoke it as well as the animals.

As Adam moved on to the next, a red roan with white splashed across its rump and a bay colt at its side, Joel's gaze slid back to Elan. "Where are Meksem and the others?"

She nodded to Meksem in the distance, mounted on a stocky spotted horse Joel hadn't seen before. "She brought the herd with the braves."

Joel couldn't help sending a sideways glance at Elan. "Does she always do everything the men do?"

The corners of her mouth played, but she kept her gaze forward. "Not everything."

A chuckle slipped out, but the act brought a fresh stab of pain in his gut. He barely kept himself from gripping his belly.

"French and Caleb are with my uncle." She motioned toward a cluster of men near the center of the small village. "They plan another hunt, I think."

Another so soon? "Do these people not have enough food for the winter?" Perhaps this wouldn't be a good place to stay out the remaining cold months. Or maybe they could help bring in more meat for the people. Was there enough game in the winter that their help would justify the extra mouths they'd be adding?

The merriment faded from Elan's face. "The camas root harvest was good, but the salmon not plentiful."

He nodded. He'd noticed those two foods made up the lion's share of what these people ate. Both took some getting used to, both in taste and the way they didn't settle well on the stomach —he'd learned that from the camas Elan and Meksem had shared with them on the trail. Thankfully, he'd not been fed either of the foods since they'd reached this place. At least that was one good thing about being shot in the belly.

He glanced back at Elan. "Hopefully, they'll find a herd of elk on the hunt."

She dipped her chin in agreement, but the worry lines at her eyes didn't soften. What would she do if he reached up and stroked the skin smooth? Jerk away from him, probably. Maybe he could ease her angst through words instead.

"We'll do everything we can to help, Elan. I know the others will, and me, too, as soon as I can sit a horse. Tomorrow mayhap." He threw in that last bit as a tease. The way his belly burned more by the minute, he'd be doing good to walk again tomorrow.

She jerked her gaze to his face, eyes widening in what looked almost like fear. "You must wait. Heal first."

He'd wiped away the worry lines, but the panic creeping onto her face was worse. He reached for her hand and gave it the gentlest of squeezes. "I'm jesting, Elan. Please don't worry." Did she take her responsibilities as his nurse so seriously? Or did she feel for him even half the respect and attraction that had taken deep root inside his heart?

Her expression eased, and from the way her chest rose and fell, she looked to be trying to regain firm hold of herself. This caring spirit was one of the things he loved most about her. But how hard it must be for her to open herself to care about others after she'd already experienced so much pain in losing the family she loved.

If only there were something he could do to help her. To soften the pain from her loss and make her way forward easier. He still held her hand, and he raised it now to his lips. The act might earn him a sound slap, but if it didn't, maybe she would feel through the gesture what he couldn't say.

Surprise widened her eyes, like a doe startled in a field. But no fear mingled in those pretty dark orbs.

Good.

A motion at the corner of his gaze jerked his focus from her face. Lautua jumped up from his seat by Elan's foot and darted toward the horses, barking fiercely as he ran. A section of horses on the far side of the herd shifted, milling restlessly. Lautua sprinted in that direction, like a bullet from a gun, darting through the middle of the horses.

One of the distant animals whinnied, a high-pitched nicker that contained a note of fear.

Joel started in that same direction, but the pain in his belly kept him from breaking into a run. Lautua didn't cease barking even as he wove around horses' hooves. The animals trotted away in his wake, and his ruckus drew the attention of two mounted braves riding at the edge of the herd.

"Lautua!" Elan called out for the dog as she strode toward the horses.

"Elan, wait." He increased his speed, but each step plunged a new knife into his gut. He clamped a hand over his middle to hold his insides in place.

Elan didn't stop, which meant he couldn't either.

In the distance, one of the men wheeled his horse and spurred the animal toward the agitated horses just as one of them jerked its head up, eyes wide. The horse loosed a frightened neigh and reared, then struck out with its hind legs.

A yelp sounded in the distance. Lautua? No, the dog couldn't have reached the other side of the herd yet.

The horse spun and charged its attacker, teeth bared and ears flat against its head.

Elan screamed and charged among the horses, weaving through them.

"No, Elan. Come back!" Joel's heart pounded against his aching ribs.

The herd was more than restless now. Lautua's constant barking setting them all on edge. Elan could be kicked or bit or trampled by any of them.

But she didn't stop.

The brave charging on horseback yelled a high-pitched war cry as he reached over his shoulder and drew an arrow from the quiver tied on his back. He fit the arrow into a bow he must have had attached to his saddle.

Within less than a breath, he raised the bow to sight, drew the fletching back, and released the arrow.

The horses blocked Joel's view of his target, but the spot where the man aimed was farther away than Elan or the dog. The brave drew another arrow and shot, then another.

Joel reached the herd himself now and plunged between two horses. He gripped his belly with both hands, hunching over to ease the fire inside. But he had to keep his head up so he didn't lose sight of Elan. Had to keep his wits about him so he wasn't trampled.

The horses on the far side had turned frantic with piercing whinnies and cries of pain. One of the animals spun to kick out at its attacker. Wolves? That was the only predator he could think of that might attack such a large herd in the light of day. Lack of game would make them daring.

Lautua must have reached the attackers, for his barking erupted in a fierce dogfight. A cacophony of snarls and barks and howls almost drowned out the scream.

Elan.

She hadn't reached the far edge of the herd, but she'd increased her speed. Probably frantic to save her dog. Did she have a weapon? The knife that always hung at her waist, but probably nothing else.

For that matter, he only had his hunting knife, too. But he had to get to Elan. She was charging right into a wolf attack. How many were there? The brave was still shooting arrows and had almost reached the fray. The other brave who'd sent his horse racing to the melee was shooting also.

And Meksem. A wave of relief slipped through him. She was farther away but ducked low on the back of her galloping horse, fitting her own arrow in her bow. She would make sure Elan stayed safe.

The awful sounds of the dogfight still filled the air. Cries of animals in pain—he couldn't tell if they were from the wolves or Lautua.

The first brave had reached the group now and leaped from his horse, swinging a hatchet and raising fierce screams as he charged the beasts.

Elan was almost there. *God, don't let her be hurt.* When all this was settled, he'd find time to have a real talk with the Sovereign instead of these desperate pleas, but for now, he desperately needed Divine help to keep Elan safe. And the dog. If she lost the pet she'd become so attached to, how much would that set back her grieving?

Don't put her through that, Lord. Please.

Just as she reached the fighting animals, the brave released a long shrill cry as he charged one of the wolves out of the herd. A flash of gray appeared in front of the Indian, a wolf darting for cover in a few trees lining what must be a creek.

Elan had dropped out of sight, and panic surged through Joel at not being able to see her any longer.

But as the echoes of that final war cry faded, no yelps or barks rose up to take its place in the quiet.

Only the snorts of a few horses. The murmur of voices. The second brave had reached Elan now and dismounted.

Joel could just see her head now, bending over something on the ground. His gut knotted, twisting with his pain as bile tried to force its way upward.

But he couldn't let his body stop him. Had Lautua been killed? Only one wolf had been chased away, but so many arrows had been shot. How many had been in the pack? The horrible noises had sounded like at least five or six. If they'd all converged on Lautua, the dog wouldn't have stood a chance.

Meksem reached the group just as Joel was pushing past the last horse. He slowed long enough to take in the sight before him.

The carnage.

CHAPTER 16

*J*oel swept his gaze around the area. Blood covered the snow, glaring red against the dirty white of ice crystals stomped into mud. Wolf bodies lay like rocks rising up through the snow. Six at first glance.

The horses had spread out in a semicircle around them. Several with their heads low, blood smearing their chests and legs.

But Elan was his focus, as well as the brown form lying on the snow in front of her.

Meksem dropped to the dog's other side, so Joel moved to his head. When he bent to lower to his knees, his stomach sent a shot of agony through him so fierce, he nearly fell face-first on the ground.

He grabbed at whatever he could to keep from landing on the dog. His hand closed over Elan's shoulder, and she gripped his arm, helping him lower to his knees.

As the pain ricocheted inside him, increasing with each round, he worked to make his breathing shallow. Anything to keep from putting pressure on his belly. A buzzing sounded in his ears, blocking out all other sound as his vision turned gray—black at the edges.

If only he could roll on his side and curl around his belly to stop this agony, but he didn't dare move. Didn't dare breathe anymore. Maybe this was the end. Death would almost be a blessed relief from this miserable torture.

Almost.

At last, the shooting agony eased. His vision cleared, turning from almost colorless to an overly-bright view, as though he were peering through a window with the sun glinting intensely enough to partially blind him.

The ringing in his ears lessened but didn't go away completely.

He strained to hear what the others were saying. They were speaking in their native tongue, and with his mind so fuzzy, he couldn't decipher any words. But as he forced his eyes to focus on the dog, some of the fog muddling his thoughts faded away.

The pup lay stretched out on his side, eyes open, head on the ground. But at least he still lived. Blood coated his front shoulder and a back leg. So much sticky red made it impossible to tell exactly what his wounds were. But the glassy sheen in his eyes proved the pain he was in.

Joel knew the feeling well.

The women had stopped talking, and only then did he realize Elan was looking at Joel, studying him. Probably seeing the pain he was struggling to keep pressed down.

He struggled to think of what he should say. "How is he?"

Her gaze shifted to the dog. "I think a broken leg. Many wounds. Need go to lodge."

The dog was big enough she might have trouble carrying him the distance. But Joel wasn't sure he could manage it either. He'd be doing well to get himself standing and walk back under his own strength.

Maybe the two women together could manage the dog. Or... where were the men?

A glance up showed the two braves were looking at one of the horses, and another man was riding toward them, as well. They probably had their hands full taking care of the horses' injuries. And most warriors wouldn't concern themselves with a pet, not when the business of the tribe also needed seeing to. The wolf carcasses would need to be dressed also. At least the animals could provide food for the people.

"I help you." Elan pushed up to her feet and reached for Joel's arm. The last thing he wanted was for her to feel obligated to assist him, for him to be so weak that he had to depend on others. But her touch worked its usual magic, easing his pain and filling him with an extra bit of strength.

He worked his way up to standing, and, as his head spun from the fresh press of pain, her hands steadying him might have been the only thing that kept him from toppling.

At last, the spinning slowed, and he eased out a slow breath. "I'm all right."

He worked for a smile to calm the worried lines in her expression, but his own face wasn't obeying the command. Maybe words would distract her. "Want me to carry him?" He would have nodded toward the dog, but every movement tightened the knife twisting his belly and made his vision wobble.

"I'll do it." She ducked down to crouch beside Lautua, and Meksem helped her load the animal into her arms.

The two spoke quietly in their language, then Elan rose and turned back toward camp.

Meksem must have freed her mount, for she walked along with them, moving horses out of their way as needed. For his part, the pain made him focus on each laborious step, but the helplessness was driving him mad. Maybe he shouldn't have come charging out after Elan. He'd only worsened his wound and hadn't done anything to help her.

But he wouldn't have been able to watch her handle the herd and the wolf attack and the injured dog without at least being nearby. He'd once thought he wouldn't be happy until he could finally be on his own, not struggling under the weight of responsibility for someone he loved.

It turned out, he wouldn't be happy on his own after all. The longer he knew this woman, the more he couldn't stand the thought of not being near her. Of not giving everything he had to make sure she was safe and happy.

And just now, that meant also protecting the dog who'd become so important to her.

～

*E*lan fought to keep the tears locked inside as she knelt beside the dog and rubbed a wet cloth over his blood-matted fur. Lautua lay with his head resting on the soft pelt she'd placed him on, pain clouding his eyes as he watched her.

"I'm sorry, boy." She murmured the words as she squeezed clean water over a wound. The flesh underneath glared at her, but with steady treatment, all the gashes should heal.

The leg would be another matter. She glanced down at where Joel knelt by the broken limb, tying off the leather wrap holding a stick in place to secure the bone.

"There. We'll need to keep him still for a while." He stroked the dog's rump in the only spot not bloody. "Think you can handle that, boy?"

Lautua's tail thumped on the packed dirt floor, but he didn't lift his head. Watching the poor dog in so much pain pressed a weight on her chest. Why did the ones she love always get hurt? Alikkees and Chuslum, then Joel, and now this sweet pup who'd worked his way into her heart with his unwavering devotion. If she could take any of their pain on herself, she would in a moment.

A hand rested on her shoulder, strong and steady. She glanced up into Joel's face, his eyes watching her with such earnest concern, a lump welled in her throat.

"I think he'll make it, Elan. Don't you?" His thumb stroked her shoulder with a touch so gentle, she wouldn't have thought a man could be capable of it.

A burn rose into her eyes as she thought through each of Lautua's injuries. She nodded. He would live, as long as the wounds didn't fester. "But his pain."

Joel must have seen how close she was to the raw edge of her emotions, for he gave a gentle tug on her shoulder, pulling her toward him. She went willingly, letting him enfold her in his arms. The tears she'd been fighting rose up anew, and she pressed her eyes shut to hold them back. One slipped down her cheek, but she focused on soaking in the comfort, the strength of him.

How long had it been since she'd been held? Comforted like this? After she'd lost her sweet daughter, after her world had shattered, the other women had spoken kind words. Meksem had listened the few times Elan let herself talk about her pain. But no one had slipped an arm around her. None wrapped her in an embrace so consuming, there was no room left for the pain that had wrecked her heart.

She inhaled a long, shuddering breath. Even Joel's scent soaked through her like a warm fire on a cold night. Musky and comforting.

For long moments she snuggled against him. But she couldn't stay there forever, as much as she'd like to. Summoning a strengthening breath, she pulled back.

He loosened his hold but kept one arm around her shoulders.

She looked down at the dog so Joel wouldn't see her face, both the red that surely rimmed her eyes and the flush already heating her cheeks. She shouldn't have stayed in his arms so long. His comfort had been too alluring.

"Elan." Joel's warm voice pulled her gaze upward, no matter how she tried to resist its draw. His eyes were just as warm. "Part of what I love about you is the way you care so much about others. You give all of yourself into tending anyone who needs help."

She couldn't breathe as his gaze held her, pulled her in to its soothing depths.

"It's a gift, but I know how much harder it makes things for you. You risk more pain than others." His hand crept up to her face, brushing her cheek. The warmth of his fingers sent a sweet sensation all the way through her, and she couldn't help but lean into his touch.

She'd never been caressed with such reverence, such gentleness. Her heart ached with the painful pleasure of it. And by Joel. Somehow, she'd let her respect for him weave deep into her heart, turn to something more. She didn't dare try to name it. She only knew this man had become as important as anyone had ever been to her.

And now, he was looking at her as though he would take away every bit of her pain if she'd let him. If only she could.

His gaze wandered over her face, lingering on her mouth. A new kind of awareness crept through her senses. Would he? Did she want him to?

He neared, his breath caressing her face. She inhaled his nearness, her eyes drifting shut. A yearning tingled in her chest, something she'd thought never to feel again.

Then Joel's lips brushed hers, the contact awakening her senses with the first touch. Her body drew strength, kissing him back, communicating what she couldn't with words.

He responded, pulling her closer, giving what she'd not even realized another person could offer. She'd never been so cherished, so treasured, as his kiss made her feel.

Joel.

He pulled back long before she was ready to stop, and she couldn't help but move closer even as he pulled away. Her heart cried out for more, but she forced herself to rein in her wayward body, the emotions left exposed.

The sting of tears burning her eyes wouldn't be held back this time.

Then Joel moved close again, wrapping her in his arms, holding her close. Rocking her as her sobs finally came. She couldn't say for sure what all she cried for. The pain. The loneliness. The utter bleakness of life without her baby girl.

He held her forever. The sobs wouldn't stop. Not until her strength ebbed, her body spent. Still he held her, tucking her head under his chin. Stroking her hair.

What a mess she'd made of herself. Of them both.

Whatever good he might have thought or felt about her before had surely been obliterated by her tears, along with the walls she'd built up to press down her grief.

Joel eased back, putting enough space between them for him to put a finger under her chin. He lifted her face, but she tried to pull away. He shouldn't see her like this. Could she have no dignity left?

"I've never met a woman as strong as you." His eyes pierced her with their intensity. Their earnestness. "It takes courage to risk loving, yet you do it for everyone around you. You're a wonder, you know that?"

A laugh slipped out before she could stop it. How could he say that?

The corners of his mouth curved in a gentle smile. "Thank you for trusting me." He brushed a finger across her jaw, then pulled back, gathering himself. Giving her space.

"Now." He turned to the dog. "What can we do to make him more comfortable?"

CHAPTER 17

*J*oel had to fight to keep from closing his eyes under the warmth of the winter sun as he sat just outside of their lodge. But the toddler hitting his leg with a pinecone wouldn't allow him rest.

"Hey, there, fella." Joel reached out and eased the toy from River Boy. "See if you can catch." The lad waved chubby hands in the air, his brows drawing together in the start of a wail. "Ho there, don't cry. Catch." Joel tossed the pinecone into the child's lap, and the frown instantly turned to a wide, toothy smile.

Joel couldn't help a chuckle.

From beside him, Elan's soft laugh spread warmth through his chest.

"Now throw it back." He held out both hands for the boy to give back the makeshift ball, but the lad pounded it on Joel's leg again.

"Nope, throw it." He took the lad's wrist and helped him make a throwing motion. Of course the little guy didn't release the toy, but he did loose a giggle so adorable Joel had to fight to keep in another laugh. "You have to let it go, you rascal."

He made the throwing motion again, and this time River Boy's belly laugh doubled him over.

Elan's chuckle was impossible to resist, pulling his gaze over to her. Drawing out a grin he couldn't hold back. "No wonder his mama needed a break. This one is cute enough to wear a body out."

"He is." Elan wore her smile in her tone. Even the dog stretched out beside her thumped his tale in the dirt. Lautua was hobbling around now, not putting weight on his splinted leg but still trying to keep up with Elan. For he was enjoying the rare winter sun with the rest of them.

"You two aren't allowed to have all the fun." Adam's voice drifted from behind.

Joel didn't turn to watch his brother's approach. Twisting still sent shots of pain through his belly. As well as bending, standing, and pretty much any other activity that involved moving his middle.

But at least he could eat more than broth now. He'd managed to keep down some of the wolf meat Elan cooked for the midday meal, and he was determined to try some of her camas cakes that evening.

If he planned to spend more time with this woman—and he *did* plan to spend more time with her, maybe even a lifetime— he'd need to learn to survive on the mainstay of her people. Smoked salmon and camas root in any form.

That didn't mean he wouldn't be thankful for real meat anytime he could get it.

"Hey there, fella." Adam dropped down to his haunches beside River Boy. He didn't even look unsteady in the act, a feat Joel couldn't help but envy. Adam seemed to be almost back to full strength.

The lad held up the pinecone. "Ba."

"Ball, that's right." Adam glanced at Joel with raised brows. "Teaching him English, I see."

Joel nodded, but he slid a glance at Elan to see if her expression showed any sign of concern. Would the mother disapprove?

Elan caught his look and nodded. "Good to learn."

Joel turned back to his brother. "His mother's feeling poorly, so Elan offered to watch him for the afternoon."

"Well then." Adam extended a hand to the boy, palm up. "Throw the ball?"

River Boy flapped his arms once, then plopped the pinecone into Adam's hand.

"How in the...?" Joel shot Elan a pressed-mouth look and shook his head. He wasn't actually jealous his brother had gotten the boy to throw the ball, but, honestly, how did Adam always manage to charm people so easily?

The cockeyed grin on Adam's face proved he was reading Joel's thoughts, but he kept his focus on the boy. "Good. Now I throw to you."

With only a few tries, he had the lad throwing and catching. And the way River Boy cackled each time, it was impossible to be miffed with either one of them.

At last, the child seemed to grow tired of the game, for he jumped up to his feet and started off.

"Wait." Elan laid aside the moccasin she'd been stitching and started up.

Adam waved her down. "I'll take him for a walk. You sit and play nursemaid to my brother."

Joel snorted. He needed a nursemaid as much as he needed another shot in the belly. But if Adam was willing to entertain the lad for a while, he'd take a few moments alone with Elan.

She paused halfway to standing, her expression showing she wasn't sure whether Adam could handle the duty or not.

Adam, of course, hadn't waited for her permission, just started after the lad with a whistle.

"He can manage the boy. For a little while, at least." Joel

touched her arm, and Elan turned that uncertain look on him. "We lived beside a large family back in Spain. The moment Adam stepped outside, the young ones would gather around him and harass his every step. He has a way with children."

Elan settled back into her seat on the ground beside him and took up the moccasin. She sent him a sideways look. "Not every boy sees past fun to what is better."

Her words crept into his chest and soothed all the jealousy away. And the gentle smile that played at the corner of her lips made him want to lean over and press his mouth right there. To share her smile until they were both grinning from ear to ear.

Right here in front of the lodge probably wasn't the place to do that, but he glanced around just in case the path all the way down the row of lodges was empty.

No such luck. And the tall, broad warrior striding toward them certainly wouldn't let him get away with a kiss in plain daylight.

A hint of a grin twitched in Beaver Tail's eyes as he neared, like maybe he knew what Joel had been contemplating. Or maybe this was simply his way of commenting about seeing the two of them together outside the lodge, enjoying each other's company. Like maybe they were a pair.

Joel leaned a little closer to Elan and raised his brows at his friend.

As usual, Beaver didn't waste words with small talk. He looked to Elan and spoke with both English words and Indian sign. "A group of riders are coming from the north. Nimiipuu." He glanced at Joel. "Nez Perce."

Elan rose in a single fluid motion. "Are they Pikunin clan?"

"I don't know. Your uncle rides with others to meet them."

Elan scooped up the leather pieces she'd been working with, then cradled the dog in her arms. "Where is Meksem?"

"Hunting."

If only Joel could stand so easily. He kept his seat on the

ground, trying his best to look like he planned to stay there. Rising would involve rolling onto his knees like an old man, then a great deal of pain and grunts as he worked himself up to his feet. Best to accomplish the job when these two weren't watching.

But Elan's nurturing tendency was too deeply engrained for her to leave him outside, even though she was clearly excited by the coming of people who might well be friends or family. Or maybe that wasn't excitement lining her face. But this news certainly had her rattled.

She paused at the door of the lodge, her hands full of leather and dog, and turned to him. "I come back to help."

He motioned her on with a smile. "I'm coming."

Elan nodded, her soft expression saying she understood. He had no doubt she'd be listening for groans or any sign he needed her to come running.

~

*F*our, no five new riders.

Elan strained to make out their faces. Clad in furs as they were, she could only discern shapes. A weight pressed on her chest as she realized she'd been looking for Chuslum. He wouldn't be riding into camp, not ever. But her father's outline wasn't among the newcomers either. Who then?

As they neared, she made out two of the younger braves from her village, one of them a son of the principal chief. Another was one of the older men who'd been friends with her husband. And two brothers who were known as fierce warriors, yet too reckless and daring in her mind.

She waited with her aunt and a few others from the Kannah village as the group rode in. Only the chief's son showed a glimmer of surprise when he spotted her. One of the brothers—

Alahmoot, she was fairly sure—guided his horse to her with a fierce scowl.

"Meksem is with you?"

Elan worked to soften her surprise. "She is hunting." The man had never given her friend much notice before, and she knew for a fact Meksem despised him. Both of the brothers. She said they were too brutal in battle and wasted too many useful parts in the animals they hunted.

He grunted. "There is news of her sister."

Elan straightened. "Telípe?"

Meksem's father was Salish but her mother Nimiipuu. After Meksem's father died when she was a young child, her mother had brought her to the camp where she and Elan had met. The Nimiipuu man her mother soon married had raised Meksem, along with the sister and three brothers that came shortly after. Elan could still remember the four stair-stepped heads following her and Meksem everywhere they went in their youth. Even when they tried to sneak away from the ruckus of the village.

But it seemed only a winter had passed when Telípe grew from that tagalong half-sister to a full-grown woman, stitching her wedding clothing. Then the Salish brave she married took her to his own village—the same camp where Meksem had been born. Where she'd spent her first five winters.

Where she'd lost the father she never spoke of.

Did Meksem begrudge Telípe the chance to live happily in the place that held so many memories for herself? Meksem had never said such to Elan, but she sometimes wondered.

And now...something in the man's face didn't look like the tidings would be pleasant.

Elan's chest tightened. "What is the news of Telípe?"

The man's scowl twisted into something like a sneer. "Captured by Blackfoot dogs. With three other women from her camp."

Fear pressed hard on her. "Captured? Not killed?" Being taken prisoner by that tribe was often worse than death. She'd heard awful tales of being kept as slaves and forced to suffer all manner of cruelty, and sometimes being sold to other tribes and taken far, far away. Never a chance to see their home or people again.

"Taken north across the mountains. A war party set out to reclaim them."

Her chest ached for what those women must be suffering. And Meksem...she would be furious. Elan's mind scrambled to piece together the full picture of what had taken place, and what might still need to be done. "When?"

The man held up twin fingers. "Two sleeps ago. They came in the dark. Her husband leads the group that has gone to catch them. Except..." Lines furrowed across the man's brow. "He is not well." He gripped his belly to show the nature of the man's sickness. "Has not kept much down for a full moon and longer."

The beat of Elan's heart surged. The man had been sick for longer than thirty sleeps? He must be weak as a child by now. Telípe's hope for freedom was in the hands of a group led by a sick and feeble man.

Meksem would want to go after them. As surely as Elan was breathing, she knew beyond a doubt—Meksem would set out at first light.

No. Elan couldn't let her go alone. Especially not after Meksem had left everything to travel with Elan when she needed her. Now was the time to be that same kind of friend.

But Joel. How could she leave him? Would he still be here when she returned? What if the journey proved deadly? So much could go wrong with two women setting out to attack a Blackfoot raiding party and free their prisoners. And if they were successful, who knew how long until they could make it back to this camp. Maybe not even before warmer weather.

Maybe... But that was too much to ask. Joel was still healing from a gunshot wound. And he'd just found his brother. There was no way he'd leave Adam again to accompany her north. They'd have to cross the mountains again if they didn't catch up with the captives first. She couldn't ask him to go.

So that meant she had to make a decision—stay with Joel or be the friend Meksem needed. How could she turn her back on a lifelong friend, especially with everything Meksem had done for her in her darkest days?

The right choice was clear, but the severing in her heart felt all too familiar.

~

"I'm going with you, Elan."

She stared at Joel, the determination locking his jaw as he stood outside the lodge. Meksem had just confirmed what Elan knew would happen—she'd be heading out at first light. She'd gone to barter for enough rations for the journey, leaving Elan to tell Joel and the others the news.

She motioned toward Adam, standing a little behind his brother. "What of Adam? You just found him." And Joel's wound. Could he ride for days on end with the way his belly still pained him? He tried to hide his suffering, but she could see through his attempts.

"I'll go too."

They both spun at Adam's words.

He propped his hands at his waist. "You'll need help."

Joel nodded as he turned back to her. "I'll bet Beaver will go too. Maybe he can even talk the captors into letting the women go. He might know them."

She sucked in a breath. Would he do that? Surely not against his own people.

"Might know who?" Beaver Tail's deep voice rumbled from behind her, and she almost cringed.

Joel didn't look at all surprised as he glanced past her to his friend. "The men who just rode in brought news of Meksem's sister. She was captured by a Blackfoot raiding party, from the north, they think. We're leaving at first light to see if we can catch them."

As much as she didn't want to turn and see the look on the brave's face, her body succumbed, moving closer to Joel when she turned, as if she needed his protection.

Beaver didn't wear the usual mask every brave learned. Instead, his expression looked...she couldn't find the word for it. Stricken, maybe. A deep sadness settled in his dark eyes.

Susanna stepped up beside him, her gaze sending a question around their group. When Joel gave her the same short explanation, a gasp slipped from her, and she pressed a hand to her chest. Her other hand gripped her husband's arm, as though she needed his solid presence.

Beaver Tail moved that arm to wrap around her waist, pulling her to him, even as his gaze turned distant, taking flight to a place far, far away.

A lump rose up in Elan's throat. Not only from the obvious pain the news brought them both, but also from the way they took comfort from each other. Could she ever have been that way with Chuslum?

A warm hand settled at the small of her back. Lightly. Tentatively. As though he thought she might not want his touch. Might not be ready for the reassuring strength of knowing she wasn't in this alone.

The burn in her throat rose up to her eyes. More than anything, she needed that touch. Needed him by her side. Ever since she'd lost the two people most important to her, she'd tried to keep herself apart. Tried to keep from risking her heart, but the effort to stay alone was almost as hard as bearing up under the loneliness.

No more. She was done fighting herself. If Joel ever gave her the chance to choose him, she would.

Susanna straightened, clearly working to pull herself from whatever thoughts had caused the sadness on her face. "If we're leaving at first light, we'd better do some cooking."

Elan almost laughed. Ever practical was Susanna.

The woman stepped forward and took Elan's arm. "You'd better help me with the camas bread. The last time I tried to make it didn't go so well."

As Elan allowed Susanna to lead her into the lodge, a smile tugged at her lips. Who would have thought that, when she and Meksem had set out on their trek to reach the great river, she'd find a friend like Susanna?

CHAPTER 18

*E*lan couldn't shake the unrest churning inside her as she sliced camas roots to make the bread. The journey ahead would be treacherous, she had no doubt. The trail would be difficult, especially if they didn't catch up to the war party before they reached the mountains. And the effort to free the captives might become deadly. For any of them.

She swallowed down the awful thoughts and reached for another root. She had to get her mind on something that wouldn't start a fresh knot in her belly. Like their food preparations. "These would be better if we had time to bake them."

"If we start them now, would they have time to bake enough through the evening?" Across from her, Susanna worked through her own pile of roots.

Elan shook her head. "Need at least one sleep, better two."

Susanna looked up and scrunched her nose. "Guess we don't have time for that."

"We have the salmon Meksem and French were able to trade for. And we can hunt as we ride." Her people had survived on much less.

But the horses. They were just now recovering from traveling through the mountains with so little food. Could they manage another journey so soon? Maybe she should try to trade at least a few of them for rested Palouse horses.

"What of the horses?" Susanna had gone back to focusing on her knife slicing the bulb, but she must have heard Elan's thoughts.

"Maybe trade for fresh horses before we leave."

Susanna looked up again. "Could we do that?" Her brow wrinkled. "I'm not sure it would be an even trade. And we don't have much to offer besides." She paused, and the distant look in her eyes showed her thoughts were far away. "I know God will provide."

The certainty in Susanna's words raised an old, familiar yearning in Elan's chest. Maybe this was her chance to ask more about her God. She swallowed to bring moisture in her mouth, then worked to make her voice casual as she focused on guiding the knife through the camas root under her hand. "Tell me about your God, Susanna. Who is He?"

The other woman's gaze weighed heavily on her for long moments. "What would you like to know?" Susanna's voice had gentled, growing almost thick, maybe with emotion.

"What does He require of you? And does He really help when you call to Him? When you..." She grasped for the word she'd heard used. "...when you pray to Him?"

"He doesn't require anything of us except that we believe in and love Him. And in return for that love, He gives us so very much. His stronger love and strength and..." She seemed to search for words. "It's hard to describe. He's so powerful. He made the earth and has the ability to do anything He wants, yet He cares so deeply about *every one* of His creations. About me, and about you, Elan. He wants you to know Him. To love Him with your whole heart."

The words Susanna spoke wove their way through Elan, but the earnest intensity in her tone drove them so much harder. *He gives us so very much. His love and strength and... He cares so deeply about every one of His creations.* That seemed like something her grieving heart would make up just to ease the awful heart-rending pain.

Could what Susanna described be real? She needed time to think.

But she might not have a chance to talk like this with Susanna again, and one question still tugged. "How do you come to know this God? How do you let Him know if you want to believe in and love Him?"

A beautiful smile spread over her face. "That's the easiest part. Just accept God's love for you. Believe that he sent His son to die a horrible death so you could have a new life serving him. Place your life in his Hands and choose to live for Him. He'll give you a fresh start as His daughter. He's just waiting for you to ask."

A fresh start. She'd never wanted anything so much as those beautiful words. The idea seemed too wonderful to be real.

⁓

*M*aybe Joel had more of his brother in him than he'd thought, because the idea of riding north on a mission to save Meksem's sister sent a thrill through his veins.

Not that he wanted any of the captive women to suffer, nor did he want anyone hurt in the battle that might take place. But the excitement, the purpose for the coming months, the chance to do something to make a difference, these filled his veins with a burn that squelched the pain in his belly.

He tied the leather strap around the bundle of foodstuffs,

then placed it on the stack with the others. That should be everything they could pack tonight. In the morning, they'd only need to roll up bedding, saddle the horses, load the packs, and hit the trail.

Holding his breath to keep in the pain, he worked himself up to standing. The move was still so awkward, lifting up to all fours first, then walking his hands up his legs until he could straighten. At least no one was in the lodge to watch him.

He'd best go outside with the others and say farewell to the friends they'd made here.

An icy wind slammed his face as he stepped outside, and he pulled his coat tighter around his neck. Beaver had predicted more snow tonight. He could only hope it would stop before first light. But if they had to ride through falling snow, at least they'd be on flat ground for a few days.

He could still remember the sensation of rolling down the mountain on his horse, ice and pain pressing on him with every revolution, weight so heavy his body felt like it might burst.

He blinked to push the memory away. The fading light made it hard to distinguish details, but the cluster of people at the edge of camp must be the gathering to say farewell.

As he approached, his eyes found Elan first, as they always did. She was speaking to her aunt and uncle. They seemed like good hardworking people, although he'd not had much chance to come to know them.

Elan looked up at him as he approached, and the softness in her expression sent a warmth flushing through him. Even in the dim light, he couldn't miss the look that made him feel as though he mattered. As though she saw deep inside him, all his flaws, his intensity that made him so focused on his mission that he didn't always react well to distractions.

But Elan seemed to see past all that to the reasons why. His need to protect. He felt a responsibility to make sure nothing bad happened to those in his care.

He stepped up beside Elan, soaking in the way her presence always made him feel like the better version of himself. He had to force his focus from her face and onto the Indian man and woman standing in front of them.

Her uncle watched him with a stoic gaze, not giving away any emotion. That probably meant he didn't approve of anyone who might think of taking the place of his deceased nephew. Especially not someone like Joel, who surely wasn't as big and strong as her husband had been.

Before he could chase down that thought, a movement from the corner of his gaze tugged his focus. A figure ran toward them.

"Pikun-hazual!" The woman's voice sounded desperate, and wasn't that the same name Elan had called River Boy? This woman might be the lad's mother.

Elan separated from the group to meet her, and Joel moved in behind her. He couldn't understand the quick murmured conversation between them, but when Elan whirled away, her eyes held a fear that gripped him.

"River Boy is missing." She grabbed his hand and almost pulled him toward the others.

He motioned Beaver Tail and Susanna toward them as he called out, "Caleb, French, Adam." The three looked up, then left the group of braves they were speaking with, men who'd been part of the hunting party. As they gathered around him, Meksem stepped up on Elan's other side.

With everyone gathered around, he filled them in quickly, then glanced at Elan. "Any idea where he is?"

"She has looked all around their lodge. She fears river again. Or horses."

Her words tightened the knot in his belly. Either place could be deadly for a two-year-old. He turned back to the others. "Beaver and Susanna, you check the horses north of camp where ours are penned. French and Caleb, can you check the main herd?" Then he looked to Elan. "It might be best if you and Meksem help her keep looking here in camp. Maybe he went in another lodge. Adam and I will go to the river."

He watched Elan to make sure she understood what he said, and her confident nod eased that worry. She really was a wonder the way she'd picked up the English language so quickly.

He gave her hand a final squeeze as they all spread out. Elan immediately moved to the worried mother and touched her arm as she leaned close to speak. The gentle confidence that cloaked her, especially in an emergency, would help the woman.

Now, they just had to find the boy.

He turned back to where Adam had been standing, but his brother had already started into the darkness.

Joel followed him. If the lad had gone to the river, every second could make the difference in saving his life.

$\sim$

"*T*he river's frozen. Do you think he crossed over?"

Joel gripped his belly with both hands as he struggled to keep up with Adam, clamping his jaw tight to hold in the pain radiating through him. He wasn't much help in the search, tagging along behind his brother. The least he could do was not slow him down.

Adam stood on the bank, hands propped at his waist, scanning the area around him. "What do you think?"

"Call him." Joel grunted the words through his clenched teeth. That was all he could manage. He couldn't draw enough breath to yell the boy's name himself.

Adam cupped his hands around his mouth and hollered, "River Boy!" His voice echoed over the icy river and the plains beyond.

Joel did his best to quiet his heavy breathing so they could both hear.

From the village behind them, the faint barking of a dog sounded. Lautua? Maybe. There were a few other dogs in the village, so it could have been any of them.

Another noise drifted to him. Faint, but it sounded like it might be coming from across the river. Or maybe that was only the echo of the dog.

"Call him again." The hope trying to burgeon in Joel's chest wouldn't be denied.

Adam's voice rang out again, even stronger than before.

When his echo faded, another voice rose in reply. A small tone, yet definitely not Adam's. And definitely coming from across the river.

"Come on." Adam motioned as he started forward.

"Go on ahead of me." Every moment mattered. "I'll be right behind you."

Adam reached the river's edge and slowed to step onto the ice.

A new fear clutched in Joel's chest. "Check the ice first."

Adam was already toeing a spot, pushing down with part of his foot. "Feel's solid."

Joel reached his side and peered down. If his gut didn't feel like it was tearing open, he'd drop to his knees and inspect the ice. "I don't see any bubbles that would make it weak. We need to go slowly and test each step."

Joel scanned the bank for a good stout stick. "Here, use this to test the ice before each step." A young box alder had been knocked down by heavy ice, it's base splintered so it was barely connected to the stump. The trunk was almost as thick as his wrist, and a few twists broke the wood off in his hand.

He passed the pole to Adam. "Be careful." Then memory of their reason for crossing rose up. "Hurry." River Boy must be stuck somewhere, or he would have come at their call, surely.

Adam stepped farther onto the ice, tapping with the pole before he took each step. Joel let him move several strides ahead before he started out so they spread their weight over a wider section of ice.

Each step felt like he was walking blindfolded off a precipice. Any second, the ice could crack, dropping him into the icy river. Water surely so cold a man would die within scant minutes.

Adam could die.

Fear clutched in his chest. "Wait, Adam. Let me take the lead. We can't risk you falling in and getting sick again."

But his brother was lengthening his stride now that he'd passed the middle of the river. "Don't worry, Joel. I can do it." He barely touched the pole down now before each step.

Joel did his best to increase his own speed. His foot slipped, and he threw out a hand to catch his balance. How did Adam manage such a pace? Joel focused on his footing, and the next time he looked up, Adam had reached the far side and took off in a run.

"River Boy!" Adam called, even as he ran as if he knew where the child was.

A small cry rose up in answer. Yes, Adam was moving the right direction, but it was hard to tell how much farther ahead the boy was.

When Joel reached the far bank, he eased out the long breath that had tightened his chest and followed Adam with as quick a pace as he could manage. He still had to hold his gut with both hands to keep his body from screaming through every movement.

About twenty strides ahead, Adam reached a cluster of brush at the river's edge. He ducked down, and the sound of his murmurs drifted through the darkness. A cry rose up from the boy, tinged with a little pain, but nothing like he'd have uttered if he had a broken bone or some other severe injury.

Joel eased his pace. He needed to get to them and help, but surely Adam had reached the boy in time to save him from anything that would threaten his life.

Soon, they'd have the lad back in his mother's arms. Joel turned to look toward the camp, where fires shone through the cracks between lodge coverings. They needed to call off the hunt. He could shout and maybe be heard, but better to wait until they got the lad back across the river.

Just as he neared Adam's crouched form, his brother straightened and stood, lifting River Boy up to sit on his hip.

"How is he?" Joel touched the boy's back.

Adam turned to him, River Boy pressed against his side, head tucked in the crook of Adam's neck. "His foot broke through the ice, then stuck there." Adam lifted the boy's left leg. "It's wet, but I can't tell how long he's been like that. Let's get him back where he can get warm."

A whimper sounded from the boy, and Joel rubbed his hand across the boy's back, then reached down for the wet foot. Bits of ice still clung to the moccasin, the leather turning crisp as it froze in the icy air.

"Let's go." Joel stepped aside and motioned for Adam to go on ahead.

They moved back down to where they'd crossed the river, the only spot where the brush allowed access on both sides of the bank. He did his best to stay with Adam, but the fire in his belly had spiked again. If he was going to manage a full day in the saddle tomorrow, he'd better pace himself.

By the time his brother stepped onto the ice, Joel had fallen a dozen strides behind him. He pushed himself harder. He might be needed again when they reached camp, so he couldn't take too long to get back.

His first step on the ice nearly sent his moccasins out from under him. He scrambled to stay upright, then took the next step more slowly. Ahead, Adam had almost reached the center of the river, the boy in his arms making his outline bulky against the backdrop of light from the village. Barking sounded again in the distance.

A crash ripped through the air. Then a scream. A man's yell. Adam's form dropped to his knees on the icy surface.

But not to his knees.

God, no! A splash sent Joel's blood racing through his veins, and he charged toward his brother.

One of Adam's arms waved as he struggled to keep his upper body above the ice. *The boy.*

Joel slid to his knees a couple strides before them, fighting down the grunt that forced its way out. "Adam. Take my hand."

"The boy." Adam thrust the crying lad toward him.

Joel dropped down on his side and took the lad's hands, staying as far back as he could from the weakened ice. At any moment, the surface underneath him could shatter too. *God, help us.*

River Boy's wails merged with splashing as Joel pulled him close. Adam was trying to climb out of the water, but the ice kept breaking under him.

Joel rolled with the lad away from the broken area, then set him up on his feet and pushed him toward the shore nearest the village. "Go." He gave the boy's back another push.

The lad toddled forward, amazingly, headed toward the distant shore and the lodges beyond.

Joel turned his focus back to his brother. Where was the stick? Every time Adam tried to latch onto the ice edge, it broke under him.

He spun and peered into the darkness on both sides of the bank. Adam must have dropped it when he picked up the boy. Joel didn't have time to go look.

The part of the ice that seemed strongest was on the east side, nearest the village. Joel crawled in a wide berth around his brother to get to that spot. Then he dropped to his belly again and reached out to his flailing brother. "Take my hand."

The chunk of ice under Adam's left arm broke, dropping him deeper into the water on that side. He scrambled to the right, away from Joel and toward the place that still supported his right arm. That ice cracked too, splintering under his elbow.

"Adam, take my hand!" Joel inched farther out.

Finally, Adam seemed to hear him. He shot a look Joel's way. "It won't hold." More of the ice supporting him broke away, and Adam gasped, splashing to keep himself above the water's surface.

A yell built up in Joel's chest, but he forced his voice to stay reasonable. "Take my hand *now*."

Adam looked at the ice under Joel again, as if measuring, then released his grip on the ice and plunged toward him. The hole in the ice had grown wider than his arm span, so he swam a stroke to reach the edge where Joel's hand waited.

When Adam's fingers pressed into Joel's palm, he gripped him tight, then used his other hand to grab onto his brother's wrist.

"When I pull, try to come out flat on your belly." Joel tightened his grip around Adam's wrist. "Ready, go."

Joel locked his arm tight and moved backward, pulling with everything in him. Pain surged through his belly, weakening his muscles. But he clung tight to Adam and dug into the ice with his knees.

Adam inched toward him.

Water splashed as his upper body came out first, then he hooked a leg up on the frozen surface.

The ice under Adam cracked, and he started to fall.

"Roll!" Joel yelled, tugging hard and scrambling back away from the splintering crust.

Adam obeyed, rolling like a boy down a snowy hill. Within a heartbeat, he'd made three rotations over the ice, breaking loose from Joel's grip and moving quickly toward the bank the boy had now reached.

Thank you, God. Joel's entire body drooped, his panic seeping out as the pain in his middle took over. He was far enough away from the cracked ice that he could rest for a minute. He had to get to land, but his arms felt weak as blades of grass.

Locking his jaw on his pain, he commanded his arms to work, then rose up into a crawling position. He should be able to stand now that he was halfway between the man-sized hole in the ice and the bank where Adam and River Boy stood waiting for him. Adam was drenched and would be lucky if his sickness didn't come back in full force after the dunking in the icy water, especially with the frigid wind whipping at him.

Joel motioned them on. "Go get warm. I'm coming."

"We'll wait for you." Adam sounded worried.

Joel put sharp command in his tone. "Go. Get the boy to his mother."

His brother scooped up the boy. "Hurry." Then he spun and strode with quick steps toward the village.

Good. After inhaling a deep breath for strength, Joel pushed himself up to his hands and feet, then worked his hands up his legs until he was standing. He eased out the breath.

Then the ice dropped out from under him.

Joel barely had time to gasp before the frigid water closed around him, dragging him down into the flowing river. Water covered his arms as he scrambled to raise them enough to grab onto the ice edge.

Maybe pain and weakness slowed his reaction, but the icy blast touched his chin before he could grip hold of the ice.

The chunk came loose in his hand.

Something in the water struck his foot. A log maybe. Or ice. The mass knocked him off balance, and he scrambled for another hold on the surface.

The river was carrying him, bumping his head against the

icy crust. He scrambled to grab hold, to pull himself up over the hard surface.

The entire chunk broke off underneath him, the weight of his effort pushing him down under the water's surface.

Glacial water closed in every side as darkness took over.

CHAPTER 19

*W*orry tangled in Elan's chest as she stepped out of another lodge. Where could the boy have gone?

Lautua waited for her outside and jumped to his feet, tipping his head as he stared up at her. Even the dog seemed anxious.

Her gaze wandered toward the river again, cloaked in darkness now. Was it only the fact that Joel went there to search that kept tugging her that direction?

A motion caught her gaze, and she focused on the spot. Only a night shadow?

Then a voice sounded. A shout. From Joel or Adam?

Lautua surged toward the sound, barking a fierce rhythm as he hobbled on three legs and his splint. Her heart clutched in her chest, and her feet carried her forward before she even told them to move.

She wove between the lodges, keeping her gaze on the place where she'd seen the movement. When she left the lights of camp behind her, she could finally see better.

A tiny form took shape, coming from the river. Otskai's son?

The child toddled toward her as though nothing at all was

wrong. The dog reached the boy and stopped to sniff him, then took off again toward the water. Where were Joel and Adam?

A man's shout sounded from the water. Then a splash.

No. Why would Adam and Joel be still at the river if they'd found the child? And splashing couldn't be good. The river had frozen.

Her blood pounded through her ears as she ran, images flooding her mind. Adam falling through the ice. Joel reinjuring his gunshot wound as he saved his brother. Surely none of that could be true. How could two grown men be in trouble and the boy have escaped unharmed? Nothing made sense.

A shout from behind grabbed her focus, and she glanced back, trying not to slow her running. A woman was running toward them from the village. And two other figures came from the direction of the horses. Good.

She reached River Boy and dropped to her knees in front of the child. "Are you hurt?" The boy was blubbering, tears running down his cheeks and moisture glistening on his lips, but he was walking, and she didn't see blood anywhere. Probably just frightened.

More shouts came from the river. Frantic calling. Was that Joel's name being yelled? *God, no.*

She stood and motioned the toddler toward the figure running from camp. "Go to your mama. Mama is right there." She nudged his back, and he toddled forward.

Otskai called her son's name, a joyful shout heavy with all the fear she'd faced this last hour.

Elan turned her focus to the river and sprinted toward the line of the bank. When she reached the fording place, she stopped. Ice still covered as far as she could see. Where had the splashing come from?

A figure downstream was standing on the ice near the center of the river. Adam? He was at least thirty paces away, and looked to be pounding on the ice with a stick. Trying to break through?

In an instant, a horrible possibility slipped through her.

Joel? Surely he hadn't fallen through the ice, then been washed downriver, locked under the icy shell.

God of the white man. Help him! Her heart cried out the words as she turned and sprinted alongside the river, higher on the bank where she didn't have to weave through underbrush.

Still, it seemed to take forever to reach Adam's position. "Adam!"

He looked up at her for only a second, then resumed striking the ice in violent blows, every part of him driving the rod hard.

"Where's Joel?" But she knew the answer, and there was no time to waste. Not even a second.

Not only could he freeze to death in that icy water, he wouldn't be able to come up to breathe. Unless he could find a pocket of air between the ice and running water, he'd smother long before his body froze.

Panic flooded her chest and throat, but she forced it aside as she scrambled for a rock. Something large enough to break through ice but small enough that she could carry.

A stone the size of her head was the best she could find. She hauled it up and started out onto the river toward Adam. When she reached him, he'd made only a dent in the ice.

"Move aside." She grunted the words as she heaved the rock up over her head, then plunged it down in the place he'd been striking.

Ice chips flew away from the spot. Adam pounced on the stone, then lifted it. "Get back. The ice is a lot thicker here, but when it breaks, you don't want to fall in."

She took a step back as he shoved the rock down again. It fell through the ice with a splash, Adam's hands going in with it.

He stopped himself and crouched beside the hole, reaching for his pole. "I think Joel's still upstream. This spot was narrow enough and the flowing water is only under this section, so I'm praying it washes him through here. It's the only thing I know to do."

Oh, God. What were the chances Joel would be washed to this exact spot in the wide expanse of river? Adam began whacking the crumbling edges of the ice, widening the hole.

Awful, horrible desperation welled up inside her, nearly choking off her breathing. She was going to lose Joel. Just like she'd lost her baby girl. And her husband. She never should have let herself love him.

No, God. I can't do this again. A fierce anger boiled up inside her. She couldn't let Joel die. And if God loved her as much as Susanna said He did, He wouldn't let her lose another person she loved.

She dropped to her knees and started clawing at the edges of ice, breaking off chunks. She barely felt the frigid water splash her hands.

Adam had stopped beating the ice and moved upriver, staring intently into the ice. Looking for a dark spot that could be Joel's body, no doubt. She scrambled to her feet. She should have been doing the same.

She started toward him, but then paused. If Joel floated by their hole, someone needed to be there to snag him.

She had to stay there. To be ready to reach for him.

Dropping to her knees, she positioned herself on the downriver side of the hole where she might be able to see him coming. The liquid was clear enough she could make out shadows at least halfway down. Would he be able to stay near the top, breathing air? How long before he froze to death?

She had to force her spinning thoughts away from the awful possibilities. "How did he fall in?" She called loud enough for Adam to hear her from where he was peering into the ice a dozen paces away.

"I fell through the ice when I was carrying the boy. Joel got us out and I rolled to the shore. He told us to go on, that he would be right behind us. I thought the ice where he was standing was strong enough, and I knew I had to get the boy back to get warm. The moment I turned away, I heard him yell. Then he was splashing. Then...gone."

His voice cracked with the last words, and Elan's heart split at the same time. *Gone.* Her lungs wouldn't work as she struggled to draw in air.

Why had she never told Joel how much he'd meant to her? At least with Alikkees, she'd told her daughter of her love every day. Her sweet child had died knowing how much her mother cared for her. How she was the center of Elan's world. Even Chuslum had felt the effects of her opening heart in all the little things she was able to do for him.

But Joel... Did he know how much she'd come to care for him? She'd never told him, only kissed him during those few, life-changing moments. Why hadn't she spoken the words?

God of the white man, give me the chance to tell him. Her own words struck her with a force that nearly knocked her into the flowing water. *God of the white man?* How could she expect God to help her, to answer her prayers, if she didn't claim Him as her own?

Susanna had made it sound so simple. *Just accept God's love for you. Believe that he sent His son to die a horrible death...* She'd heard the stories her people told of the death on the cross, but the tales didn't include the other part Susanna had said. *So you could have a new life serving him. Place your life in His hands and choose to live for Him. He'll give you a fresh start as His daughter. He's just waiting for you to ask.*

More than anything, she wanted that fresh start. A God who was *hers.* Her heart craved to belong to a father she could trust. One she could cry out to for help. And not just in the hard times. She longed for a God she could live for. A purpose for her life.

I believe. I place my life in Your hands. Be my God.

"That might be him!" Adam's voice charged through her prayer, and she struggled to pull herself from the intensity of the moment.

Be my God. Her mind repeated the words, just to hold tight to the decision she'd made, even as she turned her focus to Adam.

He was bouncing sideways on his toes as he moved toward her, staring hard at the ice.

Joel. A surge of awareness sluiced through her, bringing every part of her alert.

"I think he's coming right for you, Elan. Get ready." With the words, Adam moved toward her and slid to his knees on the ice. He scrambled to plant himself beside her, then reached his hand down into the icy water up to his elbow. "Don't let it be a branch or a fish. Please."

Please, God. Let it be Joel. Let him be alive. Every part of her coiled like a wildcat, ready to strike the moment she spotted anything large in the water.

Then, everything happened so fast, her mind didn't have time to process.

A shadow. Her hand darting in the water. Adam crouching lower, plunging his arm into the river up to his shoulder.

The icy blast on her skin. Something hard.

She grabbed for it, her fingers brushing but not finding a grip. She scrambled again, finally grasping at something flexible.

Something heavy.

His coat? She squeezed with everything in her as she pulled upward.

Only her fingers had a grip, so she plunged the other hand in the water to grab on with her whole hand.

"I've got him!" Adam's cry sounded just as she finally had enough grip to pull Joel upward.

His head rose out of the water first, but she didn't take time to study him, just pulled with every bit of strength she possessed.

Together, she and Adam worked Joel's body out of the water completely, dragging him onto the ice.

A cry slipped from her as she scrambled to his side. "Joel."

He lay face up, his body limp. Motionless.

"No." She placed both her hands on his cheeks and lowered her ear to just above his mouth.

Was he breathing? She could hear and feel nothing, but maybe her skin was too numb from the cold. "Wake up, Joel." She straightened and smacked his cheeks, trying to bring life back into him. There was no telling how much river water he'd swallowed. "We need turn him. Get water out."

Adam worked to help her, flipping his brother like he would a tiny baby. Others had crowded around them, helping at Joel's feet as she took charge of his head. He was limp in her hands, a weight so heavy it nearly smothered her heart.

While Adam pressed hard on Joel's back, she reached for one of his hands and pulled the soggy glove off. Her own hands were icy, but maybe the heat her body made would help a little. Joel's face had paled almost as white as the ice chips.

"Is he alive?" Caleb knelt beside her, draping his coat over Joel's legs while Adam still pumped on his brother's back.

"I don't know." Just saying the words made the fear rise up again.

"Lord above, heal this man whom You love. This creation You formed and breathed life into. Breathe that same life into his body again. Bring him back to us, Lord, so he can live to praise Your mighty power and tell others of Your great love."

The prayer spread through her like a warm river, filling her with strength and renewing her hope.

Each time Adam pumped down on his brother's back, her own chest tightened. *Bring him back to us. Please.*

With a grunt, Joel's head jerked, and water gushed out of his mouth.

"Joel!" Relief sluiced through her. Alive. But then he lurched again, his body convulsing of its own accord.

She gripped his hand, and another surge of water spewed from him. How much more could there be?

His body stilled, his closed eyelids not moving. In fact, all the life seemed to have flowed out of him with the river water.

My God, please don't take him. Not yet.

"Come on, little brother." Adam pumped once more, his desperation clear in every word, every action.

A noise sounded, maybe coming from Joel.

She leaned closer. "I hear him."

Adam paused his efforts, and they all strained to hear. Again the noise sounded. Definitely a groan.

"Wake up, *heteu*. My love." She touched his cheek, willing her strength to soak into him.

His eyes flickered open, and her heart soared. He still lay on his belly, one side of his face pressed into the ice. But his eyes were open.

"Can we turn him over?" So much hope swelled in her chest, she could barely speak past the knot in her throat.

While the others eased his body over, she cradled Joel's head. His gaze wandered around the others' faces, then moved to hers, clinging to her, his eyes wide.

You're going to be fine, Joel. God brought you back to us. With the others all talking, she didn't try to speak the words. Instead, she let her eyes say them for her.

A shiver ran through his body. They had to get him warm and out of these wet clothes.

"Let's take him back to camp." Adam gripped his brother's arm. "Think you can walk or should I carry you?"

The shiver hadn't stopped, and Joel's face still looked almost as pale as before. His lips parted. "Walk."

"Help him." She rose up to her knees and gripped Joel's elbow to assist him on her side.

They helped Joel sit up. He still shook, his shoulders quivering so violently, he didn't look like he'd be able to balance on his own, even if he had the strength to stand.

"Allow me, ma'am." Caleb stepped beside her and gripped Joel under the arm. He looked at Adam. "Let's lift him."

With the men half-supporting, half-carrying Joel, they started across the ice toward the bank. All she could do was follow.

Icy wind whipped against them, stinging the hands she'd thought were numb. Imagining how cold Joel must be made every part of her ache. He'd managed to stay alive in the depths of the water, but would he die from sickness now?

A gentle arm slipped around her, pulling her close against a soft body. Susanna.

"I'm praying for him." If Susanna hadn't spoken the words near her ear, she might not have heard them through the wind.

Elan nodded. "I am too." She'd have to tell Susanna about the choice she'd made. Later, when Joel was warm and well.

He *would* recover. She had to cling to that hope. And she'd do everything she could to be God's hands and feet to help him.

ow could his body burn and shake at the same time? Joel clutched the fur tighter around him with flat hands, for his fingers stung too much to bend. It had been hours since they'd brought him back to the lodge and replaced his frozen clothes with dry buckskins, but he couldn't seem to stop quivering, although he lay on his side by the fire with a stack of furs over him. Even his face ached.

A hand rubbed his upper arm, a touch gentle enough it had to be a woman, yet strong enough to help work heat through his limbs. The presence that always soothed his raw insides soaked over him, and his eyes drifted shut.

Elan.

As the water had churned around him, pulling him down into the depths of the river, then pressing him upward to bang his head on the ice above, he'd known for certain he was dying.

He hadn't been afraid. Not of death. Not since he'd come to peace with God's sovereignty in his life. Now that he was learning to trust that God truly did love him.

But Elan. The thought of never seeing her again. Of leaving

without telling her how special she was. Even the thought of leaving her as suddenly as her other family had left. He'd cried out for God to save him for Elan.

And He had.

Elan's hand continued rubbing, moving down his back, then up on his shoulder again and down his arm, bringing each place she touched back to life.

He shifted his body so he could see her, turning so most of the front of him still faced the fire but his shoulders lay on the fur underneath. She dropped her hand from his arm and pulled back, a sheepish look spreading over her face. A glance around the lodge showed the rest of their group sleeping. Only he and Elan were awake.

"Don't stop." His voice rasped with the soreness in his throat. Maybe the onset of sickness, or maybe just his lungs needing to shake off the leftover ice from the frigid river water.

She looked hesitant but placed her hand back on his shoulder, rubbing a short path over his upper arm. As her gaze met his, the hint of fear there pressed hard on him. It didn't look like fear of being close to him. Something much deeper haunted her dark eyes.

Fear because he'd almost died? Fear of loving and losing again? He might not be able to take away her worry, but he had to try.

He slipped a hand from the fur and reached for hers, then wove their fingers together. His were clumsy from their pain and the places that still hadn't come to life after being frozen, but hers fit so perfectly.

Her face didn't register surprise at his action, nor any emotion really. Not until her beautiful eyes welled with moisture.

Oh, Elan. It took everything in him not to sit up and pull her into his arms. He might be weak still, but if the touch would help her, he'd find the strength.

But he had a feeling words needed to be said first.

They needed to talk about this thing between them. This intense attraction. The love he was fully ready to acknowledge. And his near death.

She probably wasn't ready to love again. She might need to see that he was here to stay. That he would do everything he could to be with her for many years to come. She might need time to learn that their future was in God's hands.

To learn of his faith.

A fresh pain pressed down on him. He couldn't commit to her until she shared his faith. Something that important would come between them if they weren't of the same mind.

He inhaled a breath through the pain radiating through him, keeping his gaze locked with hers. "Elan…" Where to start? How could he tell her everything that had been changing in his heart? Better to start with the most important.

She didn't move, just looked at him with those unwavering eyes.

He tightened his fingers with hers. "I need to tell you about my God. The One who saved me."

Her eyes softened, and the corners of her mouth lifted. "I asked Him many times to save you."

His heart leapt at her words, but then he stilled himself. Was she talking about the gods her people believed in? He shook his head. "I mean the one true God. The One who made us all and cares about each of us."

She nodded, a spark lighting her gaze. "My people have heard of Him for many years, but I did not know Him as my own until Susanna spoke of Him. On the ice, I knew I could not pray to him as the white man's God. He must be my God too."

His thumb stroked over the back of her hand. If only he could feel the softness of her skin there. "So you…you prayed for Him to be your God, too? You plan to serve Him as His own?"

She nodded, a radiance settling over her that made her look just like an angel.

His heart surged as joy flowed through him. He had to tell her of his own change. "He wasn't my God before, but He is now. The fall down the mountain on my horse, getting shot, almost dying in the river—only God could have saved me through all that." He studied her, letting his eyes roam over her beautiful face as his mind played through what this meant for them.

Now, he could tell her how much she'd come to mean to him. How he wanted to spend the rest of his life with her, and how he'd wait as long as she needed until she was ready for the same.

Before he could form his thoughts into words, Elan spoke again. "The other thing I knew on the ice is that I cannot fear love. Not any longer. When I find love, I must open to it without fear."

For a long moment, he lay there, staring up at her, sorting through all she'd said. Could she possibly mean what he thought? Could she be ready to hear all he was thinking and feeling? They could still take things slowly but... *Oh, God, if I questioned Your love before...*

Joel worked himself up to sitting, a feat of great pain, since his wounded belly was finally thawing too, loosing a fresh round of agony. But he had to be upright for this next part, even if he was still wrapped in buffalo robes.

He shifted his hand so they were palm to palm. Elan's focus never left his face, and he drank in her gaze. The sadness that used to cloak her seemed to have washed away, leaving behind only her gentleness, something he could sink into forever.

"I didn't expect it, but I've come to love you, Elan. You're the part of me I didn't realize I was missing. You make me come alive, make me a better man. I know..." He swallowed, his gaze dropping down to their joined hands. Then, he lifted his focus back to her face. "I want there to be more between us, but you'll likely need more time. I'll wait. As long as I need to."

Her eyes glimmered, and her mouth parted, then closed again. *Let her feel the same.* She'd not given him reason to think she would say no, except…she'd been through so much.

Even if she knew in her head she should open her heart to love, knowing and doing were as far apart as this land was from Andalusia. And he and Elan were from two very different ways of life.

A thought broke through with a jolt. Would she think he'd expect her to go east with him? "I don't…" He rushed the words so quickly, he had to stop and think what should follow. "I don't mean to take you from your home, Elan. Not unless there's somewhere else you want to go. Adam and I came west planning to live out our lives here. I want my home to be wherever you are."

Her eyes had grown watery, but the smile raising her lips was like sunshine through rain. "And my home is where you are."

Her words spread through him with joy like he couldn't ever remember feeling. A victory whoop started in his chest, but with the others sleeping around the lodge, he did his best to contain it. Instead, he lifted her hand to his mouth and pressed a kiss to her skin.

And then he used that hand to draw her closer, wrapping his arm around her waist.

She came willingly, but paused with her face a handbreadth from his own. "I never thought to be happy again. I thank God for bringing you to me."

He swallowed to clear the emotion rising in his throat. "Who would have thought He'd use an icy mountain river to show how much He loves us. To finally wash away the things holding us both back."

Her eyes shone. "He used the river to give us hope."

"Right you are." He let himself drink in her beautiful eyes a final moment, then closed the distance between them and tasted the sweet flavor of love.

EPILOGUE

$\mathcal{E}$ lan pulled herself up into her saddle, then sent a sideways look to Joel as she settled into the well-worn leather. He was fully covered in the fur coverings she'd quickly stitched for him, from the cap settled on his head down to the moccasin covers. She'd even made a pair of fur mittens with a flap that hung over the tips of his fingers. He wore his regular gloves underneath, and could reach his fingers out from under the fur flap, but otherwise, his hands would be cocooned under the warm cover.

Only his eyes weren't covered, and that dark gaze turned on her now. She couldn't help a smile at the glimmer that sparkled there. Even with every other part of him concealed, his eyes could speak all he wanted to say.

Just now they sent a warmth swirling in her belly, especially when he reined his horse toward her.

"You are warm enough?" She couldn't keep the smile from her voice. He'd fussed a little when she helped him don the furs that morning, but he was grateful for them. The kiss he'd given when the others stepped out of the lodge had more than assured her of that. He'd thanked her with words, too, of course.

"Feels like I'm tucked under a thick blanket." He stroked the wolf fur covering one arm. "I'm still not sure how you made all this in one day." Raising his eyes to hers, he gave her one of those tipped smiles that made her heart flip.

"I will need to go over the stitches again, but I can do that at nights on the trail." More than anything, she wanted him to feel loved and cared for. And keeping him warm on the journey to free Meksem's sister would accomplish both of those things, especially as he was still recovering from his night in the frigid water two sleeps before.

Meksem had agreed to wait one day for him to recover. And now that the second sleep had passed, she'd determined to ride out this morning whether anyone else accompanied her or not. Of course, Joel wouldn't be kept down any longer either.

No matter how dangerous this journey might be, she couldn't help the flutter of pleasure in her chest at the thought of spending long hours in the saddle beside him. They could have many talks—of things both important and not, of stories from the past, of dreams for the future. A single moon ago she'd not thought it possible to dream again. And now she couldn't seem to stop.

Joel mentioned having Caleb speak the marriage words over them as soon as they finished this mission to find Meksem's sister, since Caleb had been ordained by God to do such back in his hometown. A reverend, they called him. The thought inspired so much hope in her chest, she could barely contain it. More than anything, she wanted their union to be blessed by God. Pleasing to Him, just as she now craved every part of her life to be.

Yes, she could barely contain the hope for their future.

"Where can I get one of those bear suits?" Adam nudged his horse up alongside Joel's, breaking through her thoughts as he sent his brother a cheeky grin. He then shot Elan a wink that said he was teasing. She had a feeling life with him as brother would be never be dull.

"First, you'll have to find a woman as special as this one. Then you can have nice things like a full suit of furs." The smile Joel sent her stirred a new flutter in her chest. How could he make her feel so wholly loved with a single glance?

"Is that what it takes?" Though Adam's words might have been part of his jesting, something like longing in his tone made her look up at him. He sent glance toward the village. Had he met a woman there?

Joel seemed to catch it too, for his shoulders straightened and he studied his brother.

Just as Adam turned back to them, something must have caught his notice, for his eyes widened. "Would you look at that." He spoke low, almost under his breath.

Elan turned to see what he spoke of. Meksem rode toward them from the village, mounted on her mare with a spotted horse trailing her. This one had large black spots dotted over its entire body in a bold, striking pattern.

Meksem guided her mount toward Adam, deliberation marking her manner. For his part, Adam stared right back, although it was hard to tell if he was watching the woman or the horse.

Awareness settled through Elan. Was Meksem the woman who'd formed that longing note in Adam's tone a few moments before? Surely not.

But...maybe. The two didn't talk much, but they did seem to do a lot of looking at each other.

She'd assumed the unusual orange color of Adam's eyes was what made her friend study him so often. And most men hadn't seen a woman who dressed in a brave's tunic and leggings the way Meksem did, participating in all the hunting and war games with the men. She usually garnered odd looks from the braves until they became accustomed to her presence among them.

But this intensity pulsing between the two of them now was more than curiosity on either side. Meksem reined her horse to a stop in front of Adam, then extended the new horse's tether rope to him. "You have suffered much to get the spotted horse. Now is yours."

The animal snorted, wide-eyed as Meksem tugged it forward toward Adam.

He was quiet for a long moment as he assessed her. Surely he wouldn't resist. Even Elan wasn't sure why her friend would do this good thing, but Meksem was right. Adam had come too far and endured great hardship to obtain a Palouse horse. This animal she offered him was one of the nicest Elan had seen.

Without speaking, Adam dismounted from the plain brown horse he rode and stepped to the spotted gelding. He extended a hand to let the animal sniff him. The horse still held its head high, the whites of its eyes flashing as it blew on Adam's fingers.

Slowly, Adam moved his face closer to the animal, breathing into its nostrils, exchanging the greeting of the horse. The gelding relaxed as Adam reached a hand to stroke its neck, moving alongside the horse to stand by its shoulder.

After long moments, he looked up at Meksem. "Whose is he?"

She held out the tether again. "Yours."

He stared up at her, but from Elan's position, she couldn't see his eyes. She could certainly imagine their orange intensity —so much like Joel's, except a startling color.

Meksem returned his stare, yet she held her chin up in the aloof pose of a warrior.

"How did you come by him?" Adam's tone was casual as he reached up and took the rope.

"I traded for him."

Traded? Elan had been through their packs many times, and

neither of them had anything significant enough to trade for a horse like this, except maybe their own horses, which they were both riding.

Except...

She didn't realize she'd sucked in a breath until Joel looked over at her. Surely Meksem wouldn't have given the only thing she had left from her father. Her real father, the one who'd given her that final gift with his dying breath. Surely Meksem wouldn't have traded her birthright for this horse she now gave to Adam.

Meksem wouldn't look at her. Instead, she straightened her shoulders and glanced around at the rest of their group who had gathered around them. "We ride now."

Elan met Joel's gaze as they fell in line behind Caleb's packhorse.

His eyes asked what the deeper significance in the gift was.

Later. She would tell him all she knew when they were alone. After she'd pulled the details from her friend about why she would trade her most priceless possession for a horse she then gave away. What exactly was brewing between Joel's brother and her friend?

For now, she settled back in her saddle, relishing the breeze on her face as they traveled alongside the river. No matter what lay before them, as long as Joel rode beside her and God guided their way, she would no longer have to walk the trail alone.

Who knew what adventure they would be in for next? Just the thought filled her with hope.

Did you enjoy Elan and Joel's story? I hope so!
Would you take a quick minute to leave a review where you purchased the book?
It doesn't have to be long. Just a sentence or two telling what you liked about the story!

～

To receive a free book and get updates when new Misty M. Beller books release, go to https://mistymbeller.com/freebook

And here's a peek at the next book in the series (Adam's story!), Light in the Mountain Sky:

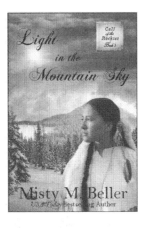

CHAPTER ONE

WINTER, 1831
CLEARWATER RIVER VALLEY, FUTURE IDAHO TERRITORY

Meksem might have made the biggest blunder of her life.

She couldn't agonize over the decision now, though. Not as her mount's hooves pounded into the pressed snow of the game trail. The thundering of her friends' horses thudded hard behind her.

If she let her mind dwell on the birthright she'd just traded away, she would lose sight of the mission before them—to catch up with the Blackfoot war party who'd kidnapped her half-sister. No matter what, she had to free Telípe from her captors and bring the girl safely back.

Telípe's husband was said to have already started out after her, leading a small group to catch up to the kidnappers and free the captives. Yet he'd been ill for over thirty sleeps, not able to keep food down. He must be impossibly weak by now.

Their mother would be beside herself. And Telípe's father. Their mother's second husband had spent many years protecting and providing for his family, but now Meksem's turn had come. Though she and Telípe shared only the same mother, the girl was family—her responsibility.

This rescue she could do. She had to.

Besides, she had a whole band of new friends to help. Maybe even too many friends. Seven, aside from her. Along with their mounts and packhorses.

How could they ride fast and sneak up on the Blackfoot with so many? She'd become accustomed to traveling with groups of warriors, but in those cases, she'd only been responsible for herself and making sure *she* didn't slow or burden the others.

Now, she owned responsibility for leading all these. She'd started this mission. It was her sister they'd set out to free. What if she led them astray? What if she led them into a trap?

She'd worked hard through the years to sharpen her senses. To perfect her aim with the bow and hone her abilities as hunter and protector. Able to match or best any warrior she came up against.

But what if all her work wasn't enough? What if *she* wasn't enough?

She'd already made one mistake that almost cost a friend's life. What if the next one proved fatal?

Locking her jaw, she pressed the traitorous thoughts aside and focused her gaze on the dark line running across their path ahead. A small river, a good place to slow the horses and let them catch their breath.

As she neared the water, she raised her hand in the signal to walk and reined her mare down from a lope. Apash shook her head and blew out a long breath as she stretched her neck. Meksem patted the mare. *You're doing well, my friend.*

She and Apash had traveled great distances together, and the horse hadn't failed her yet. Always a match to any steed the other warriors rode.

Turning in her saddle to see the group stringing out behind in the gray afternoon sun, her gaze landed on Adam first, riding right behind her. Sitting tall and comfortable on his brown gelding, he looked at perfect ease.

And his eyes. Those uncanny orange eyes always gripped her, stealing her breath and drawing her in. When she'd handed him the spotted gelding and said *Yours*, the joy that sparkled in those startling eyes had made it even harder to look away.

The moment she'd seen the animal, she'd known Adam would love him. The same glow lit both their expressions. And the horse's coloring...she'd never seen such perfect markings. Such striking contrast between the pure white background and the black perfectly-round circles. She'd seen other horses with an eye-catching coat, but the lean musculature and the excellent proportions—all of it came together in this animal to form a horse any chief would prize.

In fact, the chief she'd traded with had treasured the animal a great deal. Nothing but her most precious possession would make him give up the horse, even though he owned a full herd of others.

A burn crept up the back of her throat as an image of the jade-handled tomahawk slipped through her mind.

She forced the memory and the emotions away, jerking her gaze from Adam to scan the others behind him. Her nearest friend, Elan, rode beside Joel, who was both Elan's intended and Adam's brother. Then came the big man, Caleb, then French, the one from the north who spoke like the trappers who often wintered in their village.

And in the rear, the Blackfoot brave, Beaver Tail, with his woman, Susanna. Meksem's stomach churned at the sight of his warrior expression. She'd still not grown to be at ease around the man after spending so many days with this group. The Blackfoot were sworn enemies of both of her tribes—her mother's Nimiippu, who the whites called Nez Perce, and her father's Salish.

This Blackfoot brave hadn't seemed cruel and treacherous, except perhaps during their first meeting when he'd sprung upon her in the darkness of a cave. Even then, he'd not pressed his advantage, only forced her and Elan into daylight so they could all come to an understanding of each one's purpose.

But now... Now that they tracked a band of Blackfoot kidnappers, how could she be certain this man didn't plan to take them all captive as soon as they neared his people?

She couldn't be certain.

Which was why she would watch him. Her life, Elan's life, and even her sister's life might depend on her diligence.

Turning to the trail ahead, she adjusted her position in the saddle as her mare descended the bank to the river. The water flowed freely, but not too fast. From what she remembered, the animals would only be wet to their bellies, and the distance across wasn't more than four or five horse lengths.

An easy crossing.

Apash stepped into the freezing liquid without hesitation. The mare possessed the perfect combination of trust in Meksem's guidance, courage to face any obstacle, and savvy ability to overcome complications that sprung up.

Several steps into the water, the mare paused to adjust her balance against the steady flow. Meksem glanced back to check those behind her. Adam's riding horse had stepped into the water, but the new spotted gelding balked at the bank's edge, pulling hard on the tether rope Adam held.

He crooned to the stubborn animal, the shift of his elbow showing his steady tugs, but nothing swayed the spirited horse.

Caleb nudged his mount up behind the Palouse gelding,

crowding it so the animal might choose the more spacious option of charging into the water.

The gelding jerked its head back, half-rearing as its eyes flashed panic.

"Ho there. Easy, boy." Adam's settling voice grew louder to gain the horse's attention.

The calming words didn't penetrate the thick-headed animal's fear. The horse jerked and spun, charging into Caleb's mount as it pulled hard to free itself from the tether tugging it toward the water.

Caleb's horse stumbled from the force of the spotted gelding's blow, staggering backward. Meanwhile, the panicked horse squealed and lunged sideways, away from Caleb and his mount, ready to dart around the pair and run far from the frightening water.

"Ho!" Adam's voice rose above the melee. He held the tether rope tight as he struggled to turn his mount and follow the terrified gelding out of the water.

But the spotted horse wasn't waiting. Catching sight of a clear retreat beside Caleb's horse, he charged through the opening, jerking Adam out of the saddle.

Why didn't he let go?

Adam landed in the water with a splash, on his knees and struggling to his feet as the panicked gelding tugged him hard.

When he cleared the river, Adam gathered himself against the pull of the rope and bit out a sharp, "Ho!" He used his entire body as leverage against the fleeing horse.

The crazed gelding slowed, spinning sideways and jigging its front feet as it stared with wide eyes at the river.

"Settle down." Adam's voice shifted back to its soothing tone, although this version had more backbone to it as he took a slow step toward the horse. He kept the rope tight, but the animal didn't try to retreat from him.

In truth, the animal didn't seem afraid of Adam at all, only the river it seemed to think would surge up to eat the horse alive.

"That's enough now." Adam still advanced toward the gelding, moving hand over hand along the tight tether line as he spoke in that same calm-yet-determined tone.

When he reached the animal and slid a hand up its face to rub a palm over the flat spot between its eyes, the gelding finally dropped its head with a long sigh, giving in to the magic this man seemed to wield with animals.

Adam kept one hand rubbing the spot between the horse's eyes, then used the other to stroke its neck, working his way over the crest until he had the horse in something like a hug. The animal looked more like a lap-dog now than the crazed beast of moments before.

Adam glanced up at Caleb. "You all right?"

Caleb nodded, his hands propped over the front of his saddle in a relaxed pose as he watched Adam. "Me an' this ol' girl don't break easy."

Then Adam turned his gaze to Meksem, apology in his eyes. "Sorry for the delay."

What could she say? He hadn't meant for his horse to respond so fiercely to the river water. And *she'd* been the one to bring the animal along in the first place. She'd traded her inheritance for the gelding, after all. How could she quibble about a short delay?

But they'd never catch up with the Blackfoot at this pace. And Adam was soaked from the knees down. In this frigid air, he'd freeze. Maybe even lose some toes.

He must have seen her looking, for he dropped his focus to his feet, and a frown furrowed lines in his brow.

Then he jerked his head up. "You all go on across. Caleb, do you mind taking my riding horse with you? I think this youngster will go fine if I walk him at the same time the rest of you cross."

An uneasy churning started in her middle. She glanced out at the center of the river. The water wouldn't come to his waist, as best she remembered, but he'd be soaked. When they first found Adam in the Kannah village, he'd been on the doorstep of death from sickness. His body had burned with so much fever, he'd not awakened at all the first few days. He couldn't risk sickness like that again.

They'd have to take time to dry his clothing and warm him after he waded through the river. In truth, his leggings were already so wet they'd have to be dried. Perhaps soaking them a second time wouldn't make a difference. Either way, they'd have to stop and build a fire when they reached the other side.

He met her gaze, and his chin came up as his eyes sparked determination. "I won't hold you up any more than I already have."

Not true, but they had no choice at this point.

She turned her mare back toward the opposite side of the river and started forward again. She tipped her head just enough to keep an eye on the happenings behind her. Caleb grabbed the reins of Adam's riding horse and started through the water.

Adam led the spotted horse alongside Joel's mount and stayed side-by-side as they approached the river. The gelding paused at the edge, the whites of its eyes flashing fear and its nostrils flaring.

But then it stepped forward at the same time Adam did. The first hoof sank into the water, then a hesitant second hoof as it brought its back legs forward. The horse paused for a breath, then jerked the first front hoof up and plunged it forward again.

Step by step, the animal progressed alongside Adam, smoothing out its movements as its confidence grew. She couldn't hear Adam's low voice, but his lips moved as he spoke to the animal. Twice, he reached over and laid a hand on the gelding's neck, encouraging. The man had a way with horses, no doubt.

She could imagine exactly how the spotted gelding felt with Adam by its side. As though it had finally met someone who saw through the bluster to the fear and mistakes underneath, and looked past even those to the true being at the core.

There were times Adam looked at her that way. As though he saw both the person she really was and the person she wanted to be. The only other human who'd ever seen that had been her father.

Maybe that was the reason she'd traded her most prized possession for this horse she knew Adam would love so much. If she could give him this joy, maybe the gift would be thanks enough for the way he made her feel—fully known, and not lacking.

Except...now, the gelding couldn't be bringing much joy. Frostbite surely, but not joy.

When she reached the opposite bank, she turned Apash toward nearby trees that would provide shelter for a warming fire, then slid to the ground and started pulling out supplies. If they could get him warm quickly enough, they might cover a bit more distance before nightfall. She planned to push as far past dark as the horses could manage, but she'd have to watch the people, too.

Especially Joel, with all his injuries. She'd already shot the man with a rifle—albeit, accidentally—and she couldn't strike the final blow by wearing him out in the saddle.

Meksem moved through the copse of trees to find bark dry enough to burn. They carried dry wood with them to use in the night's fire, but they needed that for their camp later. Anything she could find for fuel now would be helpful.

"No fire." Adam's words stopped her short as she bent to scoop up a branch lying atop the snow.

She straightened and turned to where he dragged himself and the now-calm gelding from the river. Water streamed down his buckskin leggings. His breath clouded in the frigid air, which would grow even frostier as night progressed.

They had no choice. He had to dry out and get warm.

But as she turned back to her wood gathering, he motioned again for her to stop. "Give me a minute, and I'll be ready to keep riding."

Frustration swept through her. A minute was much shorter than the time it would take to build a fire, but every delay twisted inside her. If they waited very long, they may as well camp in this place. Telípe's weak and sickly husband would find her before Meksem did. And how would he overpower the Blackfoot captors?

Telípe might be lost forever.

If the Blackfoot made it back to their own territory, the girl would be condemned to unspeakable horrors.

She locked her jaw to hold in her anger. But as her mind told her to build a fire before she wasted any more time, her gaze fixed on Adam as he pulled out the furs from his bedroll.

He bent down and unlaced his tall moccasins enough to slide them off, then rolled his leggings up above his knees—then even higher, as far up as the wet leather would go. White flesh glared out at her, darkened a little by the dusting of black hairs that showed even across the distance between him. She glanced away as a heat crept up her neck. She'd seen other warriors' legs and never taken notice. Why did Adam's affect her?

Then he covered the exposed area with a wolf skin, wrapping the pelt around and around before strapping it tight with a rawhide tie. The fur enclosed the full length of his leg, all the way down to cover his foot. Not a single piece of flesh peeked out.

As he worked on the other leg in the same way, the others in their group gathered around. Everyone had made it through the river, and if they could keep Adam from taking sick, it appeared none would be the worse for crossing.

If Adam stayed well.

He'd successfully removed the wet leather from contact with his skin, and maybe the fur would keep his legs and feet warm. Maybe.

When he finished wrapping both legs, he scooped up his soaked moccasins and tied them to hang from his saddle. They'd freeze before they dried, but at least they weren't hurting anything.

He didn't even glance her way as he took up the tether for the troublesome gelding, then paused to give the horse a gentle rub between the eyes. The animal dropped its head at Adam's touch, lowering its eyelids as though the single stroke soothed away every fear. Adam's mouth moved as he spoke to the horse. He gave his riding horse a pat on the shoulder, adjusted the fur over one foot to fit it in the stirrup, then mounted in a single, fluid motion.

Finally, he turned to her with a nod. "Ready."

Sitting there atop the brown horse with the spotted one calm at his side, Adam looked as confident as any man ever could. Even the thick fur wrappings around his legs seemed natural.

She wanted to dislike him, truly she did. She was used to competing with men, not feeling any soft emotions. But when he looked at her with that gentle smile, the corners of his eyes crinkling in a way that made her feel as though he saw and knew and liked her anyway, she couldn't keep herself untouched by this man.

That fact had already proved her downfall. If she wasn't careful, much more would be lost.

Even more than the treasure she'd already given up.

Get LIGHT IN THE MOUNTAIN SKY at your Favorite Retailer!

ABOUT THE AUTHOR

Misty M. Beller is a *USA Today* bestselling author of romantic mountain stories, set on the 1800s frontier and woven with the truth of God's love.

She was raised on a farm in South Carolina, so her Southern roots run deep. Growing up, her family was close, and they continue to keep that priority today. Her husband and children now add another dimension to her life, keeping her both grounded and crazy.

God has placed a desire in Misty's heart to combine her love for Christian fiction and the simpler ranch life, writing historical novels that display God's abundant love through the twists and turns in the lives of her characters.

Connect with Misty at www.MistyMBeller.com

ALSO BY MISTY M. BELLER

The Mountain Series
The Lady and the Mountain Man
The Lady and the Mountain Doctor
The Lady and the Mountain Fire
The Lady and the Mountain Promise
The Lady and the Mountain Call
This Treacherous Journey
This Wilderness Journey
This Freedom Journey (novella)
This Courageous Journey
This Homeward Journey
This Daring Journey
This Healing Journey

Call of the Rockies
Freedom in the Mountain Wind
Hope in the Mountain River
Light in the Mountain Sky
Courage in the Mountain Wilderness
Faith in the Mountain Valley

Hearts of Montana
Hope's Highest Mountain
Love's Mountain Quest
Faith's Mountain Home

Texas Rancher Trilogy

The Rancher Takes a Cook

The Ranger Takes a Bride

The Rancher Takes a Cowgirl

Wyoming Mountain Tales

A Pony Express Romance

A Rocky Mountain Romance

A Sweetwater River Romance

A Mountain Christmas Romance

Made in the USA
Columbia, SC
06 September 2021

44990573R00111